Digital ISBN: 978-0-473-75586-7
Print ISBN: 978-0-473-75585-0
               978-0-473-75588-1

The Tale of Two Bostons

Serena Black

By Serena Black

Ten Easy Steps
The Reluctant Bride
Leonie's Christmas Miracle
The Gift of Love

Sisters & Scoundrels
The Magic of San Miguel
Taming the Golden Dragon

For Nana

Chapter One

It was at one of her favourite restaurants in New York's Little Italy that Alyssa Lee was having lunch with her boyfriend. She silently sighed knowing that if she were truly being honest with herself, Neil was just another in a long line of wrong boyfriends. He should have been given the flick ages ago, only she had been too much of a coward to do it.

"So Ally, my big party's on Saturday and since I really needed to know if Jack is coming, I went and asked him," Neil said.

The way he said the words so casually like he'd just ordered his lunch made Alyssa instantly furious at Neil's audacity. Trying hard to rein in her annoyance, she took it out on her lunch stabbing at her poor ravioli like it was the enemy. She looked at her boyfriend, her eyes blazing with anger as she fumed at Neil's underhanded man-oeuvre.

"You went to Uncle Jack and asked him? Why didn't you just ask me?"

"Don't get mad. I've tried asking you, but it seemed like you were putting me off. You know how important this party is for me. I've invited senior management and some of my more influential friends. You know I need Jack to help push for my promotion. The fact I know him is great, but to have him actually attending my party, what a coup." Neil sulked like it was all Alyssa's fault and he had done nothing at all wrong. He was the innocent party here.

Admittedly, it was true she had been fobbing him off about inviting Uncle Jack ever since she accidentally overheard Neil on the phone a few weeks ago as he waited for her in the building foyer. As she approached from behind, she was stunned to hear him talking to someone and saying all sorts of intimate things. At first, she just assumed he was talking to his mother or sister until some of the conversation became more than a little familial.

"You know I need Alyssa's Uncle Jack to attend my party to ensure my promotion. It's the only reason I'm even seeing her. You know you're the only one I love and want to be with," he said, into his phone.

Shock and disbelief flooded Alyssa at Neil's words. Needing some breathing space and a moment to comprehend what she'd just heard before she confronted him, Alyssa quickly headed into the stairwell and walked up one flight of stairs before getting into the elevator and coming down as if she was just arriving.

Any other woman, probably would have slapped Neil stupid before telling him they were over. However, Alyssa, although hurt, didn't want to be single as all her friends were either in serious relationships or at least had a carousel full of boyfriends.

Still stabbing at her poor ravioli, she wondered how Uncle Jack took Neil's intrusion. Knowing her uncle, he would have been polite, but would be telling her in no uncertain terms he wasn't attending. Not that she blamed him. Actually, she was quite surprised she hadn't already been on the receiving end of her uncle's displeasure.

Now was the time to end it. She couldn't pretend anymore, especially since Neil was trying to railroad her uncle.

"Neil, it's over. Uncle Jack and I won't be at your party," she said.

"What?" The stunned look on his face was priceless. "You can't do that. I know things have been hectic, but I was waiting for the right time. I was going to ask you to marry me," he said, trying to hide his panic.

Alyssa's first instinct, judging by Neil's shocked reaction was *liar, liar, pants on fire*, as childish as it sounded in her head.

"Well, now you don't have to. Give it to your other

girlfriend. We're done."

"Ally, baby. I don't know what you think you know or have heard, but there's no one else but you. I love you."

"Just like you love Alison and will be dumping me straight after the party? After you get your promotion? Well, now you don't have to," she said, standing and walking out of the restaurant.

As she walked she gathered her thoughts, hating the truth that she wasn't upset about Neil in the slightest, but rather, more annoyed with herself that she hadn't dumped him a lot sooner. If only she hadn't been such a chicken. However, his going behind her back to Uncle Jack was the last straw.

Alyssa and Uncle Jack had a more father/daughter relationship than that of uncle and niece. Uncle Jack was her father, Frankie's younger and only sibling. Alyssa's mother, Katherine separated from Frankie when Alyssa was two and so she had no real memory of him in her life.

While Alyssa grew up never knowing the real reason for her parents' separation, Katherine never lied about the fact she still deeply loved Frankie Lee and still considered him her husband even though they divorced.

There were only two certain things Alyssa knew about Frankie Lee. One, he was her father and two, he lived in Hong Kong or China. It was difficult to say which place or perhaps it was both since no one really mentioned it.

She had only ever spoken to her father on the phone, which as the years passed became very stilted and uncomfortable since she didn't know what to say to the man who sired her, but wasn't around to be her father.

Every birthday and Christmas without fail, she would get a present from him. When she turned sixteen, he asked what she wanted and being a petulant angry teenager because she had an absentee father, she said a top of the line car.

It turned up on her birthday and she was torn between disgust her father thought he could buy her when he didn't even really care, and excitement at getting a new car.

Katherine hadn't been very impressed and Alyssa overheard the heated conversation between her parents on the phone, but the car remained. Shortly after that, her mother had been diagnosed with breast cancer.

If any time was the time she needed a father for support, it was then. But still he didn't come. Yes, the phone calls to her mother were stepped up, but her father never turned up, showing Alyssa that she and her mother were on their own. And that's when she really began to hate her father.

One night while being so upset with her father, she went out and purposely hit a pole on the passenger side. Enough to be reckless, but not enough to hurt herself. She could never do that because her mother needed her.

Katherine was not only very disappointed, but extremely upset. Not long after the incident, Jack Lee entered their lives.

For a teenage girl whose father had only been a voice on the phone her entire life, the sudden appearance of Uncle Jack, an unwanted interloper in her life, meant his presence definitely wasn't welcome. Thus began the many yelling matches with doors constantly being slammed at his bossiness and stupid rules, where she would always accuse him of trying to be her father. The same father who didn't care enough about her to be in her life, so instead, she inflicted the pain and anger she felt onto Jack. However, through all the lashing out, she was constantly worried about her mother.

Alyssa couldn't remember how many times she eavesdropped on Katherine and Jack's conversations about her.

"You should put her into some sort of military school to straighten her out," Jack said.

"You only say that because you know I'll never do it," Katherine said.

"No, I say it because I know that one day you'll actually listen to me and do it."

"You, as well as I, know that Lys only acts like this because after never having a father around, suddenly getting an uncle trying to act like one, along with a sick mother has her feeling out of control with the world around her," she said, resigned to her daughter's antics.

Jack knew Katherine was right, yet it hurt every time Alyssa threw the fact he wasn't her father in his face, because he did love her like a daughter, even though he technically arrived on the scene sixteen years late.

One night after heavily drinking at a party, upset because her mother was getting sicker, Alyssa hadn't been in any shape to get home. She had drunk dialled her father leaving him a very angry message calling him all sorts of horrible names before calling Uncle Jack and sobbing for him to come and pick her up.

She was a mess and knew when he saw her, he was going to go ballistic. However, strangely enough he never said a thing. He just drove her home, made sure she got safely to bed and the next morning, fed her wontons in noodle soup for breakfast before taking her to the hospital to see her mother.

If there was ever a time Alyssa truly thought she would meet her father, it was at her mother's funeral. Instead a huge wreath was his only presence and if she had her way, she would have stomped all over it before burning it to ash. However, out of respect for the mother she dearly loved and her mother's undying love for her father, she very begrudgingly left it alone. That didn't mean she couldn't help scowling every time she looked at it.

About a month after her mother's funeral while she was still grieving and struggling over the loss, the subject of her father once again arose.

Since Jack was supposedly her father's younger brother, Alyssa tried to get him to explain why her father never visited or was ever present.

"Tell me why I've never met him. I mean, I don't even know where he lives or even what he looks like!" She was hoping for some kind of explanation to ease her feelings of anger towards Frankie Lee.

"Lys, as your mother repeatedly told you, it's complicated."

Katherine told her for years she would explain when Alyssa was older and now her mother wasn't around and uncle Jack was now the one fobbing her off.

"I hate you! I hate my father! And I'm sick of everyone knowing some stupid secret, but me. Why can't you just tell me?" She yelled, throwing the most childish of tantrums until he finally gave in.

"All right," he sighed, conceding defeat and making her stop to look at him. "Alyssa, even though you like to act like one, you are not a child anymore. If you really want the truth, you may have it."

Suddenly, scared and frightened of what Uncle Jack might say, Alyssa wasn't sure if she was ready to hear the truth. What happened if she heard something she didn't want to hear? All her childhood she enjoyed making up pretend stories about the man on the phone until she was old enough to understand that although he was half of her, he wasn't her father. And what about Uncle Jack? Was he even an uncle or something else? Maybe she only wanted to know because she always felt safe in the knowledge that no one would actually tell her. Was this opening Pandora's box? An instant attack of nerves made her rethink her decision.

"You know, maybe this is the wrong time, we can talk

about it later," she quickly said, walking to the door.

"Sit!"

She meekly obeyed.

"You want to know the truth about your father and mother?"

"Y-yes." She anxiously fiddled with her hands.

"It's true, your mother and father loved each other very much," he sighed, and she felt herself relax a little. "Unfortunately, what your father does — is — is the reason you and your mother are here and he, over there. It was safer for everyone."

"Wh-what do you mean?"

"I know you hate you've never met your father and you think he doesn't love you, but he does. He tried to come and see you years ago."

Alyssa's mind whirled. Was what Uncle Jack saying true, and her father had come to see her? Or was he just lying to make his brother look better in her eyes since Alyssa knew she had never met him. Even if he was standing in this room right now, she wouldn't know it was him.

"It was decided when you were two that it would be much safer for you to be here and he there, that's why you always talked to him on the phone. You seemed happy with that and there was no reason for anything to change until you got older. When you found out your mother was sick and smashed the car, he came over from Hong Kong. His first visit outside Asia ever."

"Why did I never get to see him?" Her voice betrayed all the years of hurt and pain she had kept suppressed. She was also feeling a little guilty at all the harsh thoughts she had about her father.

"Because an attempt was made on his life, so all he managed was one very brief visit with your mother before he left."

Alyssa's mouth opened and closed at the shocking revelation. It was a few minutes before she could speak.

"W-why didn't I know? She never told me. Is he all right?" She was instantly full of concern. Had her father died and she didn't even know?

"We thought it best not to tell you so you didn't get your hopes up that he'd come back or make you any angrier than you already were. You were struggling to deal with your mother's illness. It's one of the reasons why I came into the picture. To not only support both of you, but also so that you would have another family member and not be alone."

"So he's not dead?" As soon as the words came out she silently groaned at how idiotic she sounded. Of course her father wasn't dead. She begrudgingly talked to him on her last birthday.

"No, he's as well as can be."

"Why did you wait until then to become my uncle?"

"It was agreed the two of you needed to start your own life and I would just keep an eye on you both from afar. Whatever you needed, I would provide if possible."

"Our house is mortgage free. Was that you?"

"In a way. Your father bought it, but I was the one who paid for it for him."

"But you still could have been one of those uncles who popped in every now and then," she said.

"True, but it would have opened up a whole host of questions we wouldn't have answered, making you even angrier. Also, your mother and I didn't want you to accidentally think we were in a romantic relationship with each other, or that you would like us to be," he said. "No matter what anyone thinks, your mother remained faithful and loved your father every day of her life. There was never anyone else."

Alyssa sat there stunned. She remembered asking her mother why she didn't date and Katherine always said she was too busy raising Alyssa. In all honesty, Alyssa was glad her mother didn't date because she didn't want strange men coming and going from their lives, or men who thought they could suddenly become her 'father'. Now she wondered just who her father was to inspire such love and loyalty.

"So what does he do that makes him a target of assassination and won't let him leave Asia?"

Jack remained silent for a moment.

"Lyssa, you need to understand that here are Alyssa Lee, an only child of a solo mother. Lee is a common enough name which arouses no suspicion from anyone."

Her mind whirled. Was Uncle Jack going to tell her that her father was some sort of top secret spy?

"The truth and the real reason you and your mother live here and your father over there is that, he is Frankie Lee. Over there he has another name, but it's the same thing. Your father is the head of a Triad family. *That* is the reason there was an attempt on his life when he came here to visit your mother. Your father had a traitor in his organisation, which no one would ever have known about if the attempt on his life here hadn't happened."

Alyssa's mind dizzyingly spun at the announcement. Her mother loved a man who was the head of a Triad family and they were sent away because of it. It was mind-boggling to comprehend.

"S-so we were sent away to be safe?" It really wasn't the question she wanted to ask, yet was the only thing to come out of her mouth.

"Yes. At the time you were sent away, there was a lot of conflict and warring happening within the organisation and with others. Your father wasn't the head then, but nevertheless was still a member and could see the future. He loved you both too much to risk your lives or have you living like prisoners, always having to be wary and watchful, unable to freely enjoy your lives. He wanted more for you both."

"S-so are you, too?" she said, hesitant, but his chuckle relaxed her once more.

"No. Before I got too far into that, I was sent to a

foreign country by myself to get away from it all. I think my family told people I died so no one would even think twice about me being alive."

"So you haven't seen your family for years either?"

"Well, these days there's all sorts of ways to get around it, isn't there?" he grinned. "I have lots of business in Asia and see my brother as regularly as possible, bringing him news of his wild child daughter. As I shake my head in despair he would roar with laughter saying you were a chip of the old block."

For the first time since the conversation started, Alyssa smiled.

"Wouldn't people think you're related?"

"No. We started it as business dealings, which evolved over many years into friends. I make sure I'm not over there too much to arouse suspicion and it is for work. And we don't always catch up each time, or at least not in an obvious way."

"You do business with Triads? Isn't that dangerous and illegal?" she said, her eyes wide at the thought.

"No. Your father does have some legitimate business interests and I'm supposed to pretend I don't know he's actually a shady underworld figure," he laughed.

"Was mum happy? I mean, it was years since she left him and if she loved him that much..." Her voice trembled as she tried hard to blink back the threatening tears.

"I delivered to them both letters and photos. Nothing he could keep, but he appreciated seeing her and you in photos. It always made him melancholy. I think some-times he wished he kept you with him, but knew it wasn't the life he wanted for either of you. Some of his mistresses have died because of who he is."

"At mum's funeral I hated him so much for not being there. I truly believed he would attend especially since mum loved him so much. When he didn't, I wanted to take his stupid wreath, stomp on it and burn it to the ground." Her confession making her feel embarrassed by her thoughts, now realising everyone was right and nothing was like she thought.

"I know, I saw you keep looking at it in disgust. It's okay Lyssa, you weren't to know."

"How did dad take the news of mum's death?"

It was the first time in what seemed like forever Alyssa referred to Frankie as 'dad' and Jack felt a little glimmer of hope.

"Very badly. Although he was grateful he got to see her one last time. Her death hit him hard. Actually I'm going over to see him next week. Will you be okay?" He hoped perhaps now they'd had this conversation it could be some sort of fresh start.

"Of course. Will you take him a letter from me?" She bit her lip, hesitant, but it was the moment both Jack and Frankie had been waiting for.

"Of course."

Jack knew his brother was sometimes jealous when he would share stories about Alyssa. But it was the night she had drunk dialled Frankie calling him all sorts of names and how much she hated him, which tormented Frankie the most. Jack had gotten a very upsetting call from Frankie about it and as much as he wanted to go and find his niece to give her a piece of his mind, he knew she wasn't in any kind of state to understand how complicated the whole situation was.

Even now he had kept his explanation simple for Alyssa's sake, knowing how regretful and guilty Frankie felt over his daughter's animosity towards him. Would it have been better to have just kept them with him? It was a decision which tormented Frankie every minute of every day. However, he also knew he would have buried both wife and daughter long before now if he had and that would have broken Frankie.

Her letter was long as Alyssa wrote down her honest feelings and thoughts of her father from her childhood right up until the day Uncle Jack explained the situation. It didn't mean she loved him, but she liked him better. Frankie wrote back and ever since their relationship had improved and gotten stronger.

Now she was slowly walking back to work to try and clear her head after her disastrous lunch with Neil. Once she reached her desk, she had decided that after work she'd go and see her uncle and get his scolding over and done with.

"Uncle Jack! Are you here?" She called out into an empty mansion as she walked towards his home office.

Jack Lee was not only a businessman with his fingers in many pies, but also a perennial playboy and Alyssa couldn't count the number of times over the years she had caught him in some kind of compromising situation. Some a lot more compromising than others. She chided him for it, but he just shrugged and then laughed, blaming her for not making her presence known. Loudly.

Knocking *very* loudly on his office door and waiting for his answer, she heard rustling and knew exactly what she was interrupting on the other side.

"Come on in!" he said, chipper.

A woman Alyssa didn't recognise hurried out, her clothing askew.

"Uncle Jack! I called you and told you I was coming over," she scolded.

"You said a half hour. That was plenty of time," he grinned.

"You know I'm always early," she said, wondering how her uncle even got away with such inappropriate be-haviour. "You know that's considered sexual harassment in this day and age, right?"

"Of course. But believe me, if some of the stories they tell me about their boyfriends are true, then I'm not surprised they want what I can give them. I mean, even I understand no means no, and therefore all the women come to me and before we start, I make sure this is what they want."

Alyssa still didn't look convinced, but it was uncle

Jack's business and even she could testify some of the women he employed had definitely been the one to initiate sex with him and in front of her. Those images made her shiver with ickiness.

"Is it even safe to sit on this chair?" She eyed it with hesitation, not wanting to even touch it until she received an answer.

"Of course. You never want to sit in my chair or on my desk though," he laughed.

"Oh, gross. Thanks for that. Anyway, enough of your sex life, I'm sorry about Neil."

"Yes," he said, displeased. "He was very insistent I come to this party of his on Saturday. You could have warned me." Now it was his turn to scold. "He told me I had to be there because he wanted to propose to you."

Jack kept his feelings on Alyssa's smarmy boyfriend to himself. He hadn't met any of them who were worthy of her. Some he'd never met, nevertheless he still had them investigated when he learned about them, just in case.

"Sorry about that," she said, guilty. "Not to worry, you're now off the hook."

"Oh, so no engagement?" he said, breathing a sigh of relief and silently hoping his niece truly had more sense than being with a two-timing cheater. If, heaven forbid, Alyssa was so in love and actually wanted to get engaged to the moron, then he would definitely be telling her his true thoughts and opinions along with the evidence of

Neil's infidelity.

"No. We're not together anymore. He was just using me to try and get a promotion. Oh well, c'est la vie, back to the drawing board," she sighed, though not a bit sad.

"Want me to pick you out a nice man? I've got a good one who works for me, John. He's also on his way up the ladder."

"Ooh, no thanks. I've seen some of your employees and I don't know where they've been," she said, screwing up her face.

"I can tell you where the women have been." He winked, and she screwed up her face at his innuendo.

"Your company is totally off-limits. I'll find my own Mr Right, thanks. Oh, and don't you dare tell dad because I don't need another old and wrinkly seventy-year old man proposing," she giggled.

Jack had told his brother about Alyssa's terrible love life and one day, an old man mysteriously turned up on her doorstep claiming he would love to be her husband before listing the things he could do for her. Although Alyssa courteously listened, she was also disgusted by some of what he said and therefore politely as possible shut the door on him.

When she told Uncle Jack what happened, he roared so loud with laughter he was unable to control himself. Apparently Frankie thought to set Alyssa up only he hadn't realised Stan Wong was seventy.

"Your father had it on good authority from his contact Stan was a real looker, and all the ladies loved him," he chuckled.

"Maybe in the rest home," she said.

Frankie Lee hadn't been terribly impressed at his contact's idea of a boyfriend for his daughter, nor the very loud and clear, cease and desist letter he received from Alyssa telling him to go away. That she could find her own man and even if she looked for a hundred years, she didn't want either her father or uncle's help.

Chapter Two

The next day at lunch time, Alyssa exited the elevator like always and headed across the building foyer towards the entrance doors. Instinctively a shiver went through her body as if someone had walked over her grave, and although she had walked this path numerous times, right now something was different. She could feel it in the atmosphere. A strong tingling sensation of awareness throughout her body, which then hit like a bolt of lightning as her eyes locked onto another pair of intense looking caramel-coloured eyes. Suddenly it was as if nothing else was in existence in this moment.

The caramel eyes didn't feel as if their staring was creepy, quite the contrary. It was more like being cocooned in a loving warmth while also feeling almost ethereal.

"Ally," a male voice said, distracting her enough to

break the invisible thread between her and the other pair of eyes.

Mentally shaking her head and coming back to reality, she wondered what just happened. Had it even been real?

Blinking, she cleared her vision only to see Neil standing there smiling at her while holding a bunch of red roses. She wanted to groan, annoyed that her distracted state meant she hadn't seen him to be able to avoid him. He stepped forward and presented the bouquet to her.

"Ally, I'm sorry. I didn't mean to go behind your back," he said, contrite. "Listen, can we please make up and start again."

"What about your other girlfriend?"

"I dumped her. Told her it was over and you were my one true love. What do you say? Will you give me another chance?"

Feeling cornered by his appearance and question and knowing Neil would pout and sulk if she said no, Alyssa also didn't want to make a public spectacle. What she really wanted to know was if Neil really did love her, because she definitely didn't trust him right now.

"Sure, but —" She didn't get to finish because he excitedly cut her off.

"Fantastic. You're my girl again and I'll make it up to you. Listen, I have to run, I've got so much to do organising the final arrangements for my party. It starts at seven so I'll see you and Uncle Jack there, okay? Love you."

He gave her a quick peck on the cheek and then left her

standing there speechless, holding an unwanted bouquet of roses. Seeing an older lady sitting nearby, she went over to her.

"Here, you look sad. I hope these can cheer you up." She handed over Neil's roses and then walked into the sunshine smiling to herself.

Alyssa was in her pyjamas getting ready to watch a couple of chick flicks as she placed the bowl of popcorn on the table. Unsurprisingly, her phone began to ring incessantly and she ignored it for as long as possible before answering it otherwise it would drive her mad.

"Where are you?" Neil shouted, as Alyssa sensed he was only just managing to control his panic and anger at her. "You're late!"

"No, I'm not," she said, completely calm with a hint of a smile.

"You're here? I don't see you. People are asking about you," he said. "You know how much this promotion means to me. You said you'd be here."

"No, actually I didn't."

"This is *important*. It'll set me up for bigger and better. You *need* to be here," he whined.

Although she may have thought it unbecoming of a grown man to act so childish, Alyssa also knew her instincts were right to not buy into what Neil was selling. He was clearly only using her for a promotion.

"Oh well, that's life. Oh, and by the way, we're through for good."

"But Jack's still coming, right?" he said, extremely desperate.

"Goodbye, Neil." She gave a little derisive laugh.

Disconnecting the call was one of the best feelings she'd felt in ages. To celebrate she got the ice cream out of the freezer and proceeded to eat it.

Since her horrendous relationship with Neil was now over, Alyssa decided she was going to live up the rest of her twenties whether her girlfriends wanted to come for the ride or not.

The following week she went clubbing and was surprised three other girlfriends wanted to come along. They moaned they never got to cut loose anymore making Alyssa roll her eyes.

Hitting the town for a big night out, they started with dinner at an upmarket restaurant. As luck would have it, Uncle Jack was also dining at the same place and paid for their table.

Alyssa enjoyed catching up with her friends as they reminisced about the good old single days together while every now and then the talk would turn to more mundane things like sharing chores at home.

They lost Isla after dinner, saying she had drunk too much and apparently couldn't keep up these days, and so the rest of them continued on as a trio.

The club was packed with bodies pressed up against each other, which also meant that the women were also easily separated with all the jostling. While she couldn't seem to find her friends, she decided to get a drink rather than try to join the crush on the dance floor.

"Hi, can I get you a drink?" the man standing next to her said.

He looked just like the type of man she needed: handsome, great smile, well dressed, friendly and definite sex appeal.

"That'd be great, thanks!" she said.

His hand remained touching her arm while he got them a drink and Alyssa enjoyed the fact it was as if he didn't want to lose her in the throng of people.

"I'm Boston."

"Alyssa."

More than once he steadied her when she was jostled and she liked the feeling he was looking out for her.

"Quite the crush, isn't it?" he said, into her ear because it was so loud.

"It sure is," she said, shivering at his voice as her stomach fluttered in excitement.

Her friends finally found her and curiously eyed the hottie she was talking to.

"We're getting tired. Will you be all right if we leave now?" Liz said.

"Sure. You have a good night."

"You too." Liz winked.

Alyssa waved her friends goodbye and Boston leant forward.

"Want to go somewhere quieter to talk?"

She nodded and he held her hand leading her to the exit. The air outside was much cooler than the heat of the club and Boston, ever the gentleman, gave her his jacket to put around her shoulders.

"That's better. I can hear you now," he grinned. "Do you want to walk to the café down the street and grab a coffee? I'm pretty sure it's still open at this time of night."

"That sounds great," she smiled. "So what do you do?"

"I have my own company. You may have heard of it, BC Corporation."

"Wow, impressive." She had indeed heard of his company.

"What about you?"

"Marketing."

"I really want to kiss you," he said.

"Well, why don't you."

Boston's kisses were so much better than Neil's ever were, Alyssa thought. They were standing in the nearest shop doorway kissing for what seemed like an eternity and before long both were wanting more. He pushed her up against the wall as his hand lay on her thigh for permission.

A phone began ringing and they reluctantly broke apart.

"Sorry," he said, before growling down the line.

"What? Your timing sucks. This had better be important."

Alyssa smiled in amusement. She would be acting the same way if one of her friends called right now as well.

"I'm really sorry, but I have to go," he said, rueful.

"Is everything all right?" she said, concerned.

"Yes, my friend's got himself locked up in jail for something stupid, so I need to go and bail him out."

"I should be getting home anyway," she said, disappointed.

"Listen, here's my card. Call me sometime and we'll go out for dinner."

She brightened at the thought Boston wanted to see her again. Judging by the stiff white business card with embossed lettering that he handed her, Alyssa knew he had money or at least presented that look. It read: Boston Chan, Chief Executive Officer, BC Corporation.

He gave her one last lingering kiss as he helped her into the taxi, leaving her to go home alone, but at least it was with a smile on her face.

Later that week at work she was still ridiculously giggling to herself remembering her week's old phone conversation with Uncle Jack. It seemed Neil had no compunction whatsoever about calling Jack to beg him to come to his party.

"I mean, not only was he whining and begging which was very irritating in itself, but he still wanted me to believe he was planning to propose." The incredulousness in Jack's voice was undeniable. "I mean, is he that dumb that he didn't think I'd know that you weren't even there? Who was he going to propose to? A cardboard cutout?"

"Perhaps he thought you'd forget all about it once you arrived," she giggled. "So what did you do?"

"Slammed the phone down on him."

That made her laugh even harder. Serves Neil right, she thought.

To be honest, Alyssa had forgotten all about Neil since she met the charming Boston Chan who was now constantly in her thoughts. She continuously pulled out his card from her handbag and played with it. Twirling it between her fingers, wondering when would be the right time to call and hopefully see him again.

She tossed between being friendly and acting all nonchalant, just checking to see how his friend fared after being arrested, and directly asking if he wanted to go on a date. Neither option seemed like the right approach since this was the first time in what seemed like forever in which she was dying to date a man.

Previously when guys chased her, she never had much time for them because she was too busy dealing with family issues, her mother's illness, a new uncle on the scene, her absentee father issues and then her mother's subsequent death. Now she was older, she couldn't seem to find a decent man to save herself.

Although Alyssa now understood who and what her father was, which in turn helped her to understand the situation better, the thought that she could find a love like her mother and father had was hard to fathom. She wouldn't waste her life faithfully pining for some man, who had taken mistresses himself, so it wasn't like he was being just as faithful in return.

Maybe Boston would be the one to change her feelings on that, although she'd actually need to stop being a chicken and call him first.

She even thought about having Uncle Jack investigate him since she knew that's what he did with every boyfriend, serious or not. She only found out because he told her a past boyfriend was a drug user.

"Lyssa, that boy is all wrong for you," Jack said.

"What would you know, you haven't even met him yet," she said.

"I had him investigated."

"You did what?" If she was angry before, she was furious now. "What do you mean investigated? That's a complete breach of my privacy!"

"I only wanted to make sure the boys you date are worthy of you, that's all," he sighed.

"Whoa, whoa, whoa, just how many of my 'boys' have you investigated?"

"All of them."

"All of them?" The shock almost knocked her off her feet. "Bradley?"

"Yes."

"Simon?"

"Yes."

"Tom?"

"Yes, Lys, *all* of them."

"I can't believe you'd interfere in my life like that! It's…" She was so irate and flabbergasted by her uncle's devious and underhanded trick, she was speechless.

"I promise I didn't interfere. I just wanted to make sure I knew who you were dating that's all," he said, hoping she would now calm down.

She eyed him suspiciously.

"So every time I broke up with someone, you didn't have anything to do with it?"

"Promise," he said, sincere. "Except Henry. Henry, I had a word to about leaving you alone."

"Henry," she gasped. "We went out on three dates. How did you even know about him? He wasn't even my boyfriend."

"And lucky for you that's all it was," he said, ignoring her question.

"What do you mean?"

"Henry is now in jail for burglary."

"What? How do you know this?"

"Because when you were dating Henry I found out he was a petty thief. He dates women to case their houses, then he burgles them pretending all the while he's innocent. Someone caught him at it and he went to jail."

Alyssa's head spun at the information. Henry seemed so nice and she never had any kind of inkling he was a criminal.

"So how did you get rid of Henry?" She always thought he moved away, which was what his goodbye text said.

"Told him I knew his scam and there were cameras all over your apartment. And if he so much as took one item from you, I'd not only report him to the police, but I'd give them evidence of all his crimes," he shrugged.

"But that's not true," she said.

"I know that and you know that, but he didn't. Then he texted you he was moving out of town and went on to find other victims."

"You? You made him text me goodbye?"

"Well, I didn't want you moping over the loser," he huffed.

"But how did you even know to investigate Henry?" she said, bringing the conversation back around to almost the beginning.

"Lys, you know I take a very active part in your life. I watch over you like you're my own daughter."

"Do you have someone following *me*?" Even saying the accusation hurt as she shook her head unable to believe that all this time her uncle had been spying on her.

"Of course I don't," he scowled. "Give me some credit. You can have your privacy, but when it comes to your dating I just like to know what's happening."

"Then how did you know about Henry?"

"Pure luck," he grinned. "I ran into Isla and she mentioned you had a date with Henry, so I checked him out. Better to be safe than sorry."

She tried hard to be angry at her uncle overstepping the boundaries and yet, she really couldn't.

"So apart from Henry, you've never chased off any of my dates or boyfriends?"

"I swear, he was the only one."

Satisfied with her uncle's explanation she calmed down.

Learning from past history, this time she was going to keep Boston a secret for herself for a while before telling anyone. And just to be sure Uncle Jack couldn't put his nose into her business, she wasn't going to mention Boston to any of her friends either.

Chapter Three

Boston Chan was a man of many titles that he took seriously. CEO. Eldest son. *Big brother* to three younger siblings. Younger brother to two elder sisters. Okay, the last title he didn't take seriously at all, unless he was watching out for them.

As the eldest son of Thomas and Ivy Chan and third in the sibling pecking order, it was a blessing and a curse. There seemed to be a different weight of expectations on his shoulders than his eldest sister, Montana, since she was *the* eldest of all the Chan siblings. Being the third child gave him room to breathe while still having some responsibility.

All those who knew Boston, knew he was young, successful and wealthy and along with his model good looks had the world at his fingertips. After all, all the financial journalists and gossip columnists seemed to agree on these very points.

Although he was supposed to be working, he took a temporary moment to contemplate his rapid rise to the top in just a few short years, achieved through his own hard work, where he could now boast offices on both sides of the Atlantic. Sometimes even he felt overwhelmed by how he got here so fast.

He remembered the excitement of finally leaving New Zealand and heading off to London to do his OE — overseas experience — full of hope he'd have the same life-changing experience a lot of other Antipodeans had. For the first few months it had been great. The travelling, meeting new people and socialising all the time was a lot of fun, but somewhere during all that and hearing his second eldest sister, Indiana had gotten engaged, Boston began to find the constant swirl of activity tiring. He loved the travelling, just not all the drinking and partying so much anymore.

One of the perks to having two older siblings was the fact that Montana's husband, Lucas Romero came from a family who owned a lot of businesses, including a chain of hotels. Thus, Lucas got Boston a job as a porter at one of their hotels when he first arrived in London. This took the stress of finding a job away and was also a lot of fun. Boston knew this was only a temporary reprieve from finding a job in accounting, which was where he wanted his career.

When Indi moved from Canada to London to be with

her fiancé, Jason Kwong Lee, Boston had been ecstatic. Having Montana living in Italy was great, but not the same as having an actual sibling living in the same city. What made Boston's life even better was when Indi asked Boston if he wanted to live with them.

At first, Boston thought it was a strange request.

"Please Bos, I could really use your support since I don't know London and didn't really like it that much when I came over and visited Mon all those years ago," she said.

"Well, as long as I'm not intruding on you and Jason's privacy," he said, happy to give up flatting with four friends for a quieter pace.

"Of course not," she said. "To be honest, I think he'll be relieved to know that I have support, even if it does mean you living with us."

"Maybe he could buy a huge mansion and then I can live on one floor and you on another," he grinned.

"I'll let Jase know," she smiled, hugging him.

It turned out to be a great decision for all of them. While Indi and Boston got a sibling to be with, Jason also enjoyed having a 'little brother' around the house. He also wasn't as concerned about Indi if he worked late or had to travel and the two men became good friends much to Indi's delight.

Just to be sure the engaged couple had a lot of privacy, Boston ensured he still frequently socialised with friends. In fact, it was even more enjoyable for him because he could go home to peace and quiet.

Now, he was living in New York and looking out his office window at Central Park. Normally when Boston was in his office, his mind was solely focused on work unless friends or family rang, but even then his attention would shift quickly back to work. So the fact that he was currently in such a contemplative mood was out of character for him.

Knowing that since both his eldest sisters had found love and happiness, he too was beginning to show signs of wanting the same thing, perhaps not just yet but soon. He wanted his children to be as close to their cousins as possible as growing up in a large family made for some very unforgettable memories, he smiled to himself.

Somehow, he wasn't even sure if he would be able to find his future wife, what with his workaholic nature and constant travel between his London and New York offices. Yet, deep down, Boston knew if he was ever lucky enough to find the woman he wanted to marry, he would change his lifestyle so he could be a very present partner and even more hands-on father, if he was so fortunate.

Women constantly rang wanting his attention, yet no one ever held his interest long enough to become anything more than a quick fling. Then yesterday he saw a woman, who he thought was the most stunning beauty he'd ever seen. Instantly his whole body seemed to awaken as if he had been unknowingly sleepwalking through life.

Boston had been talking to his friend, Sam in the Hightower Bank building foyer where Sam worked. As they chatted Sam's attention was taken by something over his shoulder behind him.

"Who or what are you looking at?" Boston said, curious.

"The guy behind you. I see him here often. Right now he's on the phone to his girlfriend and waiting for his other girlfriend for lunch."

Sam's quiet explanation made Boston turn around to see who the Casanova was his friend was referring to. His interest now piqued.

"How do you know all this?"

"I've overheard his conversations. He gets really mad when this girlfriend isn't down here waiting for him when he turns up," Sam scowled. "He's a real piece of work."

"So how do you know he's cheating on her?"

"Listen."

It wasn't too hard to eavesdrop since the man wasn't being quiet.

"I know honey, just a little longer. I just need her to help me get this promotion and then she's gone. Yes, I know but it's her uncle who I need at the party. Believe me, I've dropped tons of hints. You know I hate doing this to you, but it's for our future, that's all. Listen, I got to go, she's coming. Love you," the man said, disconnecting his call.

Boston was shocked the man was brazen enough to tell

his girlfriend he was actually cheating on her and then for the girlfriend to actually be understanding about it all. What kind of people were they?

"Well at least one of his girlfriend's know he's cheating on her," he wryly said.

Sam gave him a nudge.

"Here comes Miss Gorgeous."

Boston turned to see the woman unknowingly being strung along and as soon as he laid his eyes on her he felt a rumble deep in the depths of his soul, which got louder and stronger the longer he looked. It was as if his whole body woke up after being dormant for years. She looked like an angel in a blue dress and seemed to float towards him with the smile so bright, it could light up cities. The rest of the world faded away. There was no building, no people, not even his friend, Sam. Just an angel gliding towards him. Her black hair was shoulder-length and her eyes seemed to shine like black onyx with a drop of warm sherry. Their eyes met and he swore he felt a strong telepathic connection.

"I love you," Boston blurted out, inwardly cringing at his idiocy.

"Pardon me?"

"I said, I love you."

"I heard you but..."

"But what?"

"I don't even know you."

"I'm telling the truth." He sounded offended she would

even doubt his words.

"No one goes around telling strangers 'I love you'. It's creepy."

"But it's true."

"Again, I don't even know you. So why on earth would you even think you loved me?"

"Because it's true."

"Bos. Bos! Hello?" Sam was nudging him.

"Huh? What did you say?" he said, noting he was back in the foyer and the woman and man now gone.

"You were off in space. I've never seen you like that ever," Sam said, amazed Boston seemed to be lost in thought.

"Sorry, just deep in thought about a problem at work. I thought I just got the answer," he lied.

"Listen, want to catch up sometime for dinner?"

"That'd be great. Give me a call."

Sam walked off and Boston, for the first time in his life, was shaken by an encounter which never actually happened.

It was this mystery woman who was now dominating his thoughts so much so that his work, which he thrived on was losing the battle, something which was unheard of. Boston knew he needed to find her, get her out of his system like he did every other woman he had ever been with so then life could go back to normal. Even the women who played hard-to-get eventually gave in to him. *None* consumed his thoughts like his mystery woman though.

He also knew the real reason for today's deep contemplation was all because somehow she had managed to not only make time stand still, but they had some kind of otherworldly conversation, which had *never* happened to him before.

Heaving a sigh, he sat back at his desk and began to push through as much paperwork as possible.

Chapter Four

Today was the day she was finally going to bite the bullet and ring Boston for a date. No more dilly-dallying, Alyssa sternly told herself. After breaking her own vow of secrecy so she could talk it over with Liz and Claire who had seen him at the club, but not before first extracting their promises not to mention Boston to Uncle Jack, they urged her to go for it.

"So, you think I should call him?" she said, anxious.

"Who?" Claire said.

"The hottie from the club?" Liz said.

"Yes, him. Boston Chan."

"Well, he was *hot*," Liz grinned.

"Why not? What do you have to lose?" Claire said.

"But what if I make a dork out of myself and he doesn't even remember me? I mean, it's been a few weeks."

"That's because you've been too chicken to do it and if you had talked to us earlier we would have badgered you to do it a lot sooner," Liz said.

"Which is probably why Lys didn't talk to us," Claire laughed.

"Then why don't you just go fishing? Mention your name and see how he reacts, then you'll know whether to ask him out?" Liz said.

"Oh no," she groaned. "I didn't even tell him my name."

"What?" Her friends looked at her in astonishment.

"You didn't tell him your name?" Liz said. "So, you smooched his face off, but remained nameless?"

"Go Lys," Claire giggled.

"Maybe you could call him and say, hi Boston, remember me? I'm your mystery woman, the one who was too busy kissing you to tell you my name," Liz laughed.

"Not funny," she groaned. "Now what am I going to do?"

"Just call him. I bet he probably doesn't even really remember you, anyway," Claire teased.

"Thanks a lot."

"You're welcome," Claire grinned. "And this is why I'm so glad I'm no longer single. I don't have to deal with all this dating angst."

"Lys, just call him, otherwise you'll just drive yourself crazy," Liz said.

Once the decision was made, Alyssa still couldn't bring

herself to actually call Boston and spent the next few days still staring at his card and fiddling with it.

"Hi Lys, I'd thought I'd call and see how it went?" Claire said.

"I'm still psyching myself up to do it."

"Would you stop being such a chicken and just do it," Claire scolded.

"Your bossy support is appreciated."

"So you'll do it? Otherwise I'll have to do it for you or keep teasing you until you do it."

"Fine," she sighed. "I know when I'm beaten. I'll do it after lunch."

"Good luck and I'm expecting an update after your date otherwise I'm telling Uncle Jack."

"Thanks for the warning. Although you won't know if or when I do manage to arrange a date," she laughed.

"At the rate you're going, I'm going to be pestering you until you let me know you've at least called and made contact," Claire said.

"Maybe I've left it too long. Maybe he doesn't remember me," she said, anxious.

"Right, and there was the matter of being nameless," Claire teased.

"Actually, I remember I did tell him my name when we first met. Although he's probably forgotten it by now," she said, glum.

"It'll be fine, chicken. Just bite the bullet and call."

"Yes mum."

Deciding this was definitely a call one needed to make on a full stomach, Alyssa left the office to grab some lunch, lying to herself that she wasn't procrastinating. She was hopeful the fresh air and something to eat would calm her nerves and put her in the right frame of mind to ask Boston out on a date. All the while silently praying he'd remember meeting her.

The day was a little chilly however, the sun was out and so she decided she'd sit and eat a sandwich in the nearby park. There were also a lot of other people out and about because of the fine weather as well.

Getting her sandwich from the deli down the road, she had just exited the shop when she thought she heard yelling. By the time she looked in the direction of the commotion, something slammed into her with such a force she was spun around and knocked to the ground.

Jack Lee received an urgent call from one of Alyssa's work colleagues saying she had been knocked over by a mugger trying to flee after stealing a woman's handbag moments earlier and an ambulance had taken Alyssa to the hospital.

Rushing into the hospital in a mad panic, he finally calmed down after being repeatedly reassured by the nurses Alyssa was not only fine with a few scrapes and bruises, but there didn't seem to be any major injuries apart from the fact she was knocked unconscious.

Looking through Alyssa's handbag to make sure she still had her wallet, phone and anything else of value, he found a white business card. Pulling it out he noted the name Boston Chan and smiled. Jack knew exactly who Boston Chan was, but more intriguingly how did Alyssa get his card, and was it for business or pleasure? Silently he prayed for the latter.

Then his eyes lit up as a devious plan began formulating. It seemed terrible to be using his niece in this state however Jack was sure his brother wouldn't let such a golden opportunity pass either. Boston Chan was the kind of man both men would want for a son-in-law: young, wealthy, ambitious, handsome and the bonus, he was also Chinese.

Jack's powers of persuasion with the opposite sex weren't legendary unless you knew him and by the time he was finished, he managed to persuade the nurse she never saw him.

"If anyone asks, can you just say I've already left on my month-long business trip," he said. It was true he would be in Hong Kong and China for a month, but wasn't leaving until tomorrow. "I know it's sneaky and underhanded, but if you saw the losers she dates, you'd understand." He was trying to pull on the nurse's heart-strings.

"Sir, I sympathise, really, but this isn't *Blind Date*. It's a hospital," Nurse Gilmour said.

"Nurse Gilmour, all I'm asking is for you to call Boston

Chan at the BC Corporation on the pretext that he's Lyssa's boyfriend. If he says you have the wrong number or he already has a girlfriend, just apologise for the mistake and then call me so I can make any necessary arrangements for my niece."

"So, you're happy for me to look incompetent?"

The disapproval on Nurse Gilmour's face was an obstacle Jack needed to overcome. If this wasn't for Alyssa he would have happily conceded defeat and not wanted to put the nurse in a more difficult position. Nevertheless, this was about his niece and the chance she could have finally found the one man on the planet both Jack and Frankie would wholeheartedly approve of, so he was willing to do anything to help a potential love match along, which included setting them up.

"Tell you what, I'll take you out for a very lavish dinner of your choice when I get back, no matter how this turns out."

"What about my husband?"

"Bring him along. Obviously if you were single I'd be telling you to bring the nurse uniform too," he winked.

Nurse Gilmour couldn't believe she actually blushed at this man's flirting.

"What if my husband and I are into threesomes or have an open marriage?" she teased.

Jack's face lit up at the flirty banter.

"Hey, whatever rocks your boat I'm happy to help. You know the old saying, *you scratch my back, I'll scratch yours* or even better, I can…" He whispered in her ear as she felt herself redden and get extremely heated.

"Oh my, you are the devil."

"Only when I'm being naughty," he grinned. "So you'll do it?"

"Yes, but only because if this works out, it'll be a great story to tell. I don't need the other stuff," she said, making sure Mr Lee got the message she wasn't going to be joining him for any kind of hanky-panky, even if it was a little bit thrilling to have him flirt so outrageously with her.

"Thank you, my darling. I am in your debt."

His fingers were crossed that by the time he returned, the two young people would at least be dating and before he flew out, he ensured a large bouquet of flowers along with a large box of chocolates were delivered to Nurse Gilmour to thank her for her assistance.

"Mr Chan?" a feminine voice in a brisk no-nonsense tone said, down the line.

"Yes, may I help you?" He was annoyed with the interruption by someone who he clearly didn't know.

"This is Nurse Gilmour. We're calling to let you know that your partner, Miss Alyssa Lee has been in an accident."

"My what?" he said, surprised.

"Is this not correct? I'm sorry to have disturbed you,"

she said, brusque.

"Wait. I don't think… I'll come and… I'll be there as soon as possible," he said, confused.

The name the nurse said didn't register any recollection with him and Boston only agreed to go just in case he might at least know who she is and could find her rightful next of kin. He wondered who they would have called, if anyone, if he hadn't said he'd be there and for some unknown reason that worried him.

Sighing, he headed off to the hospital to clear up the misunderstanding and hopefully at least, perhaps ensure the woman would get safely home. As he sat in a taxi, he wondered why this Alyssa Lee didn't tell them who her next of kin was herself, and then that dreaded sinking feeling occurred that she must not have been able. Now he was silently hoping nothing really terrible had happened to the poor woman.

Alyssa Lee. He rolled the name around in his head but there was no recognition. Admittedly it sounded like a pretty name, however it wasn't one which stood out as someone he had ever met or at least recently. He did have to some admit relief it also wasn't one of his ex-girlfriends. That was one complication he didn't need.

Turning up at the hospital still unsure if he was doing the right thing, he entered and prayed he could at least advise where she possibly worked so the hospital could then get in touch with the right people who may know her next of kin.

"Excuse me, I'm looking for Nurse Gilmour."

The pretty nurse at the nurses' station on the floor he had been instructed to go to, appreciatively eyed him.

"Oh, she's just gone off to do her rounds. Can I help?"

Her voice and the gleam in her eyes left Boston in no doubt that she meant professionally and personally however, he just ignored it.

"Yes, I was told Alyssa Lee was here."

"Oh, you're Miss Lee's boyfriend." The young nurse was crestfallen. Of course someone like him had a girlfriend.

Not wanting to be a liar, Boston ignored the comment.

"Can you tell me what's happened?" he said.

"It's our understanding that the patient was knocked down by a mugger fleeing after snatching a purse. She was knocked unconscious and an ambulance was called and brought her here," the nurse said.

"So, she's still unconscious?"

"As far as I know, yes."

Boston wasn't sure whether to be relieved or not. There was a part of him which hoped that after turning up and meeting this woman, she would realise a mistake was made and they could have a good laugh over it. However, now that didn't seem to be the case.

"May I ask how you knew to call me?"

"Sorry, I'm not sure. You'll have to ask Nurse Gilmour."

"May I go and see her?" he said.

"She's in room 102. You can go right in."

"Thank you."

Feeling like an interloper, he was still hesitant about whether he was doing the right thing or not. Perhaps he should have brought flowers or something. However, this wasn't your usual situation.

There was another patient in the room awake and he nodded and smiled acknowledging them while noting while she was also female, she also seemed too old to be Miss Lee. They also weren't unconscious unless she had woken and no one had realised. Then he read her name on the board above her head and relaxed knowing she definitely wasn't Alyssa Lee, which only left the bed behind the closed curtain.

It was ridiculous to feel so nervous, Boston told himself. He was a man who could navigate multi-million dollar deals and not break a sweat, so what was one mystery woman behind a closed curtain?

Taking a deep breath, he quickly slipped past the curtain so he couldn't think about it anymore and his eyes widened in surprise as he felt the world tilt.

The woman lying asleep on the bed was none other than his mystery woman. The woman who had given him some weird ethereal experience in the foyer of his friend Sam's building and who had been consuming his thoughts so much. Boston was even tempted to stand and wait in the building until he saw her again. He knew if he had done, then he would have also made his move, boyfriend or no boyfriend. Unfortunately, he had too many scruples to actually hit on another man's woman, even if the boyfriend was a lying, cheating scumbag.

Shaking his head in amazement and disbelief he had not only miraculously found her, but somehow she had landed right in his lap. Yes, the luck gods were clearly on his side giving him not only her name, but the assumption he was her boyfriend. Did this mean she finally dumped the two-timing cheater she was seeing? Silently he hoped so. To Boston she looked like a peacefully sleeping angel as he drank in her features. Her perfect pink rosebud mouth beckoned him to kiss her, but he didn't want to have her waken, terrified a stranger was kissing her.

His angel. Just the thought made him warm all over.

The curtain was noisily pulled back and on the other side stood a formidable looking nurse with spectacles at the end of her nose looking at him.

"Mr Chan, I presume," she said, in a no-nonsense manner he recognised from the phone.

"Nurse Gilmour?"

"Yes. Good to meet you."

"How is she?" he said, concerned.

"She took a hard knock to the head when she fell, so we're just waiting for her to wake up, which we hope will be soon."

"You don't know if the police have been called, do you?" He wanted to know if they also called any other next of kin.

"I'm not sure. Just to let you know, we did try to

contact the patient's uncle, but was told he was overseas on business for the next month," she said, and Boston didn't know whether to be relieved or not.

"Okay, thank you. I'm still not sure how you got my number?"

"Oh, the card in her handbag."

The nurse thought he was someone's partner just because his business card was in her handbag. How crazy was that? He gave them out all the time. However, since they clearly didn't know about her actual boyfriend and Boston had been wanting to find her, he decided to ignore the mistake.

"So there's nothing to do but wait," he said.

"Yes, would you like to talk to the doctor?" Her demeanour softened just a smidge.

"Please."

Nurse Gilmour walked back to the nurse's station to page the doctor thinking about the handsome young man she just left. When the patient's uncle charmed her into calling Boston Chan on the pretext his niece was his girlfriend, she gave him a firm no. However, Jack Lee was very persuasive and before she knew it, she was sympathising with the man over his niece's choice in men and agreed just this once to do this one little bit of mischief.

Upon hearing young Cassie gushing about Boston Chan, she had to go and see the hunk for herself and Cassie was right. He was handsome as sin and could only hope the young lady in the bed thought the same.

After Boston talked to the doctor, he was still none the wiser as to when Alyssa might awaken.

Alyssa. Just her name alone made him smile. Alyssa Lee. Her name was as perfect as she was. Alyssa Chan would be even better. Whoa, where did that thought come from? Boston had never entertained any thoughts of this kind before and the fact he just instinctively matched their names was worrying and yet, he wasn't calling himself an idiot, instead he felt a warmth spreading through him at the thought.

Spending as long as he could just watching her sleep before leaving, he made plans to come tomorrow, but armed with his laptop so he could at least do some work while he waited.

That night he pondered what it meant when the one woman in the world he wanted to find had somehow landed in his lap. Only she didn't know it.

The next afternoon, Boston returned to the hospital armed with flowers and a smiley face balloon, along with work.

He sat and tried to concentrate on his work, but every time Alyssa sighed, he ended up being distracted and watching her sleep, wondering if she was having pleasant dreams before he forced himself to do some more work.

Still, he was unable to keep his eyes off her for more than a few minutes at a time and then the most amazing thing happened, he swore he saw her eyes flutter, yet couldn't be certain.

"I think I saw her eyes flutter," he said, relieved to find Nurse Gilmour at the nurses' station.

"Let me just call the doctor and then I'll be right in."

Giving her a quick nod, he went back to Alyssa's bedside.

Chapter Five

Alyssa must have had a big night out last night as her head was pounding and the boom, boom, boom she could hear was deafening. Boy, did she have a headache from drinking too much. She was so tired that even trying to open her eyes was impossible and so all they managed was a shuttering before she fell back to sleep.

Now someone was being very inconsiderate and shining a light in her eyes. She mumbled at them to go away, but they clearly hadn't heard. Who did that to a sleeping person anyway? Was it some kind of prank her friends were playing on her? She tried again to tell them to go away, but all she could hear were voices ignoring her.

Something was being put to her lips and then she heard a male voice telling her to drink. Her mouth obeyed and cool water soon flowed wetting her parched mouth and throat. Her eyelids were still heavy and she ordered them to open, but once again although they tried to obey, they couldn't quite do it.

"It's okay, don't try to force it. It'll come. Just rest and sleep for now," the male voice said, as she drifted back to sleep.

Boston found himself in a panic with no idea what to do when Alyssa started waking. Her mouth moved yet no coherent sound came out. He could see her struggle and the flicker of her eyelids, yet they wouldn't open.

The doctor said these were all good signs and she'd wake when she was ready, so he went back to doing some work before leaving for the night. This time, he gave her a kiss on her forehead and she sighed with a small smile on her lips. That one small moment, not only made him smile, but he was pretty sure he may have even fallen in love.

Feeling the warmth of the sun, Alyssa couldn't wait to go outside and enjoy it. She also felt much better since her head didn't seem to ache anymore.

Opening her eyes to the world, she saw the handsomest man she had ever seen sitting beside her with a serious and focused look on his face as he stared at his laptop. Strangely she wasn't even frightened by his presence, in fact it was oddly comforting.

"Hello." She smiled as he whipped his head towards her. "You look like you're doing something very serious. Sorry to disturb you, but what are you doing in my room?"

Alyssa was finally awake with a smile which punched Boston right in the solar plexus as he felt her voice hit every nerve cell in his body, even though she spoke with the huskiness of a dry mouth. His skin prickled with an awareness he had never felt before.

"You're in the hospital. Let me get the nurse," he said, rushing away like an idiot.

Alyssa frowned. Why would she be in the hospital? Looking around the room, she realised the man was right, she was in the hospital. Before she could take stock, the man, a doctor and nurse appeared.

"So you're awake at last," the doctor smiled.

"Yes, where am I?"

"I'm Doctor Miller and you're in the hospital. What do you remember?" he said, not really answering her question like she hoped.

"Not a lot," she said, still feeling a little groggy.

"That's natural. Now, do you know your name?"

"Alyssa Lee."

"Great." Dr Miller smiled his confirmation. "Do you have any next of kin?"

"My Uncle Jack."

"Fantastic," Dr Miller said. "What else do you remember? Do you know where you live, work or even who this man is here?"

Silently watching Dr Miller pepper Alyssa with questions made Boston shift uncomfortably as he hoped she didn't scream blue murder about him.

Alyssa's head was beginning to ache at all the questions. Why did the doctor need to ask such inane questions? Looking at the handsome man, she drew a blank. Unsure whether it was intentional, but for the life of her, a name wouldn't come.

"Are you my *boyfriend*?"

The hesitance in Alyssa's voice sent a quick surge of panic through him as the doctor frowned, looking at them both.

"Are you sure you don't know him?" Dr Miller said.

Yes, Boston was pretending, but only because Alyssa had no one to care for her, he silently justified to himself. However, seeing the anxious look on her face he now felt a protective streak come over him as he gave a reassuring smile.

"I'm Boston Chan."

Nothing about his name came with any kind of recognition in her mind.

"I-I'm sorry. I-I don't know you."

Alyssa felt like she was about to burst into tears, but thankfully the doctor's matter-of-fact attitude helped her emotional upheaval.

"Not to worry. You've had a bad knock to your head. It's good you can remember your name. We'll keep you in for another night to rest. Just take it easy. Things might come back very slowly," Dr Miller said, before leaving.

Alyssa closed her eyes and Boston walked with the doctor back outside the room.

"I can't say it's serious, but it's obvious she has lost some of her memory. As I said it might come back in dribs and drabs or all at once. However, she shouldn't push it. Obviously when we release her, she shouldn't be alone for the first few days until she finds her feet," Dr Miller said.

Boston thanked the doctor and went back to sit beside Alyssa. She looked so fragile lying there sleeping and he knew he couldn't leave her to her own devices, not if she really had lost her memory. Sighing, he tried to do some more work, but found it hard to concentrate with Alyssa's sad face at the forefront of his mind. He was also torn between whether to tell her the truth about knowing him, or not. His conscience was screaming for him to tell the truth however, the little devil didn't want to because he didn't want to be sent away and not see her again.

Of course, he was being ridiculous over that. Now he knew her name, he would be able to make contact again so the truth should win out and yet, Boston still frowned in the acknowledgement that a part of him wanted to remain her boyfriend, pretend or not. The only tricky part would be if she realised he wasn't her boyfriend or she actually had one, then he would look a complete fool.

Upon his arrival the next day, she was sitting up in bed

and smiled when she saw him enter the room. To Boston, her smile could light up the whole hospital and he loved the feeling it was directed at him.

"You're looking more alert and chipper today," he smiled.

"I feel heaps better." She smiled before looking sad.

"What's wrong?" he said, concerned.

"Who are you?" She blurted out the words like it was what she wanted to say as soon as she saw him, but had managed to keep it in until now.

"Still don't know, huh?" he grinned, as her stomach fluttered.

"No and it's horrible. You're just a big black hole in my mind," she said, glum.

"Not to worry. Like Dr Miller said, your memory could take a while to come back since your bad fall," he said, sitting on the bed beside her.

Although he wanted to, he didn't dare kiss her, because she was already upset and he didn't want to add mauling her to her worries.

"How did I end up here?"

"What I was told was you were knocked down by a fleeing mugger who had just stolen another woman's handbag."

"Oh, I would have thought the hospital would have contacted my Uncle Jack," she said, confused.

"They tried, but were told he's in Asia on business for the next month," he said, thankful he knew that.

"Then you must be my boyfriend, right? You don't feel like a cousin or a brother, which I'm sure you would have said by now, if you were," she said, not adding if he was related she was definitely having an inappropriate reaction to his nearness right now.

"Of course," he said. "Did you think I just come and sit beside the prettiest unconscious patients hoping they'll wake with amnesia? Or maybe the hospital just randomly dialled a number and it just happened to be mine?"

She was torn between laughing and crying.

"Sorry, bad jokes," he smiled.

"No, don't apologise. It's just weird. I have so many questions about us. I gather I like your sense of humour?"

"All part of my charm." He winked and her toes curled.

Superficially she could see what attracted her to him and just their little banter made her even more annoyed she couldn't remember him.

"How did we meet?" she said.

It was a question he thought a lot about last night after she woke up and they knew she possibly had some amnesia. If she did get her memory back, he didn't want her to accuse him making up some underhanded lie so he went with the loosely based truth.

"You were coming out of your work elevator and I was standing in the building foyer talking to a friend. I saw you and immediately, for me at least, the whole world seemed to disappear. You looked like an angel floating towards me and I was instantly captivated by you."

He didn't mention he thought they had a telepathic conversation because she probably would have not only called him crazy, but also asked him to get away from her.

He saw her feminine reaction as her mouth opened slightly, her eyes were wide and bright and her breath had a slight gasp. Before he knew what he was doing, he leant forward to kiss her.

Alyssa's head swum. Boston's mouth was soft and his kiss tender. Her whole body felt like she knew him. Too soon he broke off the kiss to her disappointment.

Boston felt a bolt of lightning strike him. He had never experienced such a violent reaction to a kiss. If it wasn't for the location, then he would have kept going until they both reached the peak of ecstasy together.

"Is it weird to feel like we've just met and this is new for you too?" she said, her cheeks pink from their kiss.

He wanted to tell her it was the truth. They had just met and the kiss was not only their first, but it was off the charts.

"Of course not. I guess in this situation it's natural to feel like that. Tell you what, ask me anything. We'll have our first date right here, right now. Hi, I'm Boston Chan, nice to meet you," he said, holding out his hand to shake.

His offer was chivalrous and made her feel special that she had found a man so kind and considerate. It also didn't hurt he was fantastic at kissing.

"A-Alyssa Lee."

"I'm sorry we had to meet in such unusual circum-stances," he grinned.

"This is just as weird for me too. Normally I meet my dates in restaurants or cafes."

"Then we must be one of those couples who like to do things differently."

She liked the thought of that. Perhaps that's what drew her to Boston in the first place, the fact that this whole scenario wasn't run of the mill.

"Well, I think I know we live in different places," she said, hesitant.

"You remember?" He frowned.

"I think so. The image in my head doesn't scream masculine or even shared space so I'm guessing it's my place. How long have we been going out?"

"Not long at all."

"I guess that explains the separate places then," she said, disappointed they weren't living together. Every-thing in her body screamed she wanted to be with this man, especially sleeping in the same bed. That she knew him, even though her memories or lack of them, didn't. "I guess that rules out a whole lot of other questions as well. What do you do?"

"I own my own business."

"Where do I work?"

Thank God for the Internet. Knowing they were sup-posed to be dating and therefore he should know all the usual things, Boston spent last night looking up Alyssa's name on the Internet and found her company and job title.

Then this morning he actually rang and gave them an update, which they were grateful for and told him there was no need for Alyssa to rush back as people would cover for her.

"Image West in marketing," he said. "Your boss, Jon said there's no need to hurry back, that they'd cover anything urgent."

Alyssa felt more reassured by his answer than she wanted him to know, so she just nodded and silence ensued.

Her head was beginning to throb and she was unsure whether it was from trying too hard to bring back her memories or not. However, she couldn't help but feel incomplete with her amnesia. Churning the name of her boss and the company around and around in her head, she was almost blown into the bed as a rapid-fire movie played in her head. It was jumbled and the sound dubbing didn't go with the furious flickering images she could see.

It felt like someone was squeezing her head tightly because the pain, which came in short sharp bursts, was still searing and making her feel woozy and unbalanced.

"Are you okay?" he said, instantly worried at seeing the pain on her face.

"Just had a flood of memory about work. It hurts a little," she said, putting on a brave face.

Boston knew her head hurt more than she was

acknowledging, so he gathered her tightly in his arms, kissing the top of her head.

Her heart was racing as she closed her eyes and took in his scent, the feel of him holding her making her feel better.

"Is it bad?" he said. "Shall I get the nurse to give you some pain killers?"

"It's like a really bad migraine or someone squeezing my head in a vice. I guess a part of me hopes if something keeps jogging my memory then I'll put up with any pain to get those memories back," she said, as her eyes began to well up.

A few minutes later, Dr Miller came in.

"Ah, my favourite patient. I'm sad to say that you're free to go whenever you're ready, but to remember to make sure someone is with you until you find your feet. And don't forget that you still need to rest as much as possible," he said.

"Thank you, Doctor," she said.

"So when do you want to leave?" Boston said.

"Just as soon as I get packed." There was uncertainty on her face and in her voice.

"What's wrong? Aren't you glad to be leaving the hospital?"

How did she explain it? Yes, she was very glad since she was bored, but she was also afraid because of her lack of memory. She pasted a smile on her face.

"Of course, but I'll miss all the lazing around."

"Not to worry, you'll have another week of that."

Boston didn't know what to expect when Alyssa came out of the bathroom, yet she could have knocked him over with a feather. She was only wearing jeans and a blouse but to him, she looked so much younger with her clean fresh face and casual clothes.

He shook his head to himself. Having now seen three different looks to Alyssa Lee, each one seemed to captivate him even more. There was no doubting she really was a natural beauty.

Chapter Six

Boston's new top of the line Mercedes purred along and all Alyssa could do was look out the window deep in thought about her situation.

By the time he pulled up to her place, her head hurt from all the strain of trying to see what she could or couldn't remember. The good news was, at least she remembered where she lived.

"It'll be okay," he said, when he saw her pause before opening the car door.

Threading his fingers through hers, they walked to her door and he patiently waited for her to unlock it. Nervously she opened the door and the relief she felt recognising the inside was palpable. Sure she had memories, but it still scared her she might have somehow been remembering the wrong place.

Boston saw all the tension release from her body as he looked inside and saw it was very nicely decorated and furnished. It had a very homey and relaxed feeling about it.

"You sit and I'll make us a drink," he said.

"Maybe you should sit. I've done nothing but laze around in a hospital bed for days. I could use the exercise," she giggled.

"Or maybe we could do it together." His eyes darkened and before she could register anything, his lips found hers.

A soft moan escaped as she held onto him like she was drowning in his heady kiss and he, the life preserver.

"A-Ally." He moaned against her mouth and she froze before quickly pushing herself away from him.

"Don't call me that," she said, with a forcefulness which seemed foreign to her, as she crossed her arms in a defensive position.

"I'm sorry. I didn't mean to." Damn, he had now ruined a fantastic kiss by accidentally calling her by a nickname she evidently hated.

She sighed and sat on the couch.

"No, it's not your fault. I just know I don't like the name Ally. I don't know why." This overreaction was hard to understand even for her. Why had she overreacted almost violently to Boston calling her Ally?

He scrambled to think of what he should call her. What family and friends would call her.

"Lys, angel, I'm sorry. It just came out," he said, contrite and feeling like a socially inept buffoon.

Boston could see the hurt in Alyssa's eyes and didn't know if he or something else was the cause, but whichever, it stabbed at him.

"Why don't I make us that tea?" he said, moving to the kitchen to give her some space.

Coming back into the living area, he handed her a cup and prayed she didn't take sugar, but only milk.

"This is great. Thanks," she said, taking a sip of tea. "I guess you should get going, I've put you out long enough."

Boston looked at Alyssa not looking at him while she was dismissing him. Granted what she said was true. He did have a pile of work which seemed to keep growing, but for the first time ever, he wasn't in a hurry to tackle it.

It was seeing her look so lost and alone that he knew there was no way he was going to leave her here by herself, no matter what she said. It was what any good friend would do, he justified to himself, not wanting to admit he really didn't want to leave as he didn't know if he'd see her again. He was scared that if he left and she regained her memory then she'd definitely know she had never met him. He wanted to be around her when that happened so he could explain the situation, and his lying.

"Well, I do have to run home and get some stuff and now you're back home I can do some work on my laptop here. I'll grab some food as well on my way back," he said.

Although she frowned at his words, she was silently relieved he was going to stay.

"You're not staying here," she said, feeling very contradictory right now. She wanted him to stay as he made her feel safe and yet, she also felt a wariness around him. Perhaps she could call one of her friends, but then sighed. She couldn't ask them to take a few days off just to babysit her. Why did Uncle Jack have to be away right now? Once again she sighed, knowing if she rang him, he'd either return early or heaven forbid, hire someone to babysit her. Boston was probably better the devil she knew rather than some stranger.

"Of course I am. The doctor said you needed to take it easy until you find your feet. *And*, you shouldn't be alone at least for the first few days," he said.

Part of her loved his confidence that he wasn't going anywhere because she didn't want to be alone, but she was also terrified because she didn't remember him. What if he was a horrible boyfriend?

"Fine, but you can sleep in the spare room."

He gave her a look, which made her want to laugh. She could tell him he was going to be in the spare room, but the reality was, he'd be sharing her bed.

"You can't tell me that we've never shared a bed?" His eyebrows arched daring her to contradict him.

"Low blow, since you know I can't remember. What I do know is, while you may have been in my bed, you've definitely *never* stayed the night," she said, confident.

He was taken aback. Alyssa was right. He was only teasing because she couldn't remember, but the fact she could assume he never stayed the night was a slur on his name. If he truly was dating her, there was no way he wouldn't be spending the entire night with her. If any of those other jerks were dumb enough to just have sex and run, then they didn't deserve her. Alyssa was definitely a woman you stayed the whole night with.

"What makes you say that?" he said, out of curiosity and annoyance.

She smiled, took his hand and led him to the bedroom. In his head he expected a super girlie room, but to his pleasant surprise, Alyssa's room was very nicely decorated like the rest of her place. The instant he saw the bed in the room, he frowned in understanding. Her bed was a small double bed and there was no way his long frame would be comfortable in there for an entire night even if he were to hold her in his arms.

Alyssa watched Boston just shrug.

"Well, there's only one thing to do. You either move to my place or we buy a new bed. Simple," he said, as she looked at him stunned.

"You don't get to order me around. *I don't remember you*," she said, furious. "I'm guessing you've never even slept here at all because we would have had this fight before *and you would have remembered it*. At this rate, I won't be sleeping with you ever again, so you can either have the spare bed or leave." She issued her ultimatum, frustrated by her lack of memory and trying hard not to cry in front of him because it would ruin her strong stance.

Boston had been caught out and now Alyssa was irate with him. He meant his words in jest, well also a little seriously. Unfortunately, she had taken it the wrong way and now he was to be banished from her bed before he even got in there.

"I'm sorry," he said. "I was only joking but you're right, it's probably better we sleep apart." His mind and body revolted at the idea. These sleeping arrangements didn't suit him at all. He wanted to hold her in his arms and make love to her all night, but unfortunately he was going to have to give her some space, starting now.

"Look, I'll go back to mine, grab some stuff and get dinner. I'll be back in a few hours. You try to relax or rest while I'm gone."

Alyssa just nodded and sat on her bed bursting into tears once Boston left. She hated her memory loss and she hated Boston, but she really didn't hate him. She was just scared to like him just in case it turned out horribly.

Flopping back onto her bed she instinctively knew he would be an incredible lover and spending a night in his arms would be bliss. However, she held back from that desire because she wanted to know if they could get past her amnesia first. This one thing frustrated and scared her at the same time.

What if she remembered, and remembered things she

didn't like about him?

What if she didn't remember, and it just became this unmentioned hole in their relationship?

What if, she couldn't live without knowing?

What if, what if, what if. The question went round and round in her mind until it drove her crazy. Deciding to have a bath in the hopes it would not only relax her, but also calm the inner turmoil she was feeling, she sank into the warm water feeling the heat work its magic. Then she took a nap.

When Boston arrived back at Alyssa's and noted she had clearly washed, he was torn between annoyed he hadn't been here to help to ensure her safety and relieved that he didn't know about it so his mind couldn't go into overdrive at the images that would have entered his head. Although now the thought had entered his mind, he tried hard to shoo it out. He didn't need her tossing him not only out of her bed, but also out of her apartment on day one.

True to her edict, last night after a very chaste good night kiss Boston slept in the spare room, much to Alyssa's guilt because she could only imagine how it went since it was only a small single bed. However, she wasn't ready to agree to having him in her bed even if nothing sexual happened, something she knew was an impossibility as she could feel the strong chemistry between them.

Getting up after a restless night's sleep, she was surprised to find him at her dining table working.

"Good morning," he smiled. "Sleep well?"

"Yes," she lied.

"Want me to make you breakfast? I wasn't sure what you ate or how long you'd sleep so I thought I'd just do some work in the meantime."

"You keep working," she said, waving her hand. "I'll sort myself."

Watching Boston work was interesting as she could see his total concentration was focused on the task at hand as she made herself some toast and a cup of tea.

By the time ten o'clock rolled around Alyssa was going stir crazy. Normally she loved being at home just pottering around, but because Boston had invaded her space, she now felt like a trapped animal.

She tried watching TV, but nothing of any interest was on and therefore constantly channel surfed in the hopes something would miraculously pop up and grab her attention. Eventually she found a movie rerun she could at least focus on for a while.

It really didn't help the strain she felt knowing Boston was calmly sitting at her dining table working. His presence was like a big, giant immovable boulder in her apartment.

Boston couldn't focus. It didn't help that he hadn't slept a wink at all last night. He almost fell out of the bed a few times and every time he moved, a limb was hanging over the edge. He could have survived that, but for the fact only a few feet away, through two very firmly shut doors, Alyssa was sleeping peacefully like an angel. It annoyed him because he not only wanted to be sharing her bed, but doing much more in it.

Grumpy from a terrible sleep, he was now staring at his laptop trying to work, but Alyssa's presence was distracting. Every move she made grabbed his attention. Her constant changing of TV channels was irritating, but the worse thing was the fact he wanted her. This place was too small. It was like being in a cage with temptation constantly arousing you. Could his willpower be strong enough to stop himself from just picking her up and taking her to bed? And did he want it to be?

He threw down his pen in frustration making her turn to look at him.

"What's wrong?" she said.

I want to devour you, he thought before firmly shoving that thought out of his mind.

"I think I need some fresh air," he said, pushing back his chair to stand. And to put some distance between us, he silently added.

"That sounds like a good idea. Actually I was thinking of going to the supermarket," she said.

"Are you sure you're up to it?"

"Honestly," she sighed. "I'm a bit bored and could use a stretch of my legs."

He silently groaned at the image she inadvertently put into his head. He knew a great way to stretch her legs and help with her boredom. It was clearly the confined quarters making him constantly think like a horny teenage boy with sex on the brain.

"Let's go shopping. I can't honestly remember the last time I did such a mundane chore," he said.

"Really? You don't go grocery shopping?" she said, surprised.

"No. My housekeeper does it."

"This should be really interesting then," she giggled. "Let's go."

Chapter Seven

At the supermarket it was frustrating for Alyssa to have Boston with her. Not only did he seem to have every female in the store blatantly checking him out, but he liked to look and read every product on the shelves or stand and spend minutes comparing products and prices before selecting one. A ten-minute trip was turning into an hour.

"Whoa, what are you doing?" he said, as she reached to grab a jar of jam she usually brought.

"Grabbing the jam I like," she said.

"But it's not on special."

"So? It's the brand I like."

"But this is the brand I use *and* it's on special."

"Okay, we'll buy that then," she said, reaching out to grab it, but he grabbed her hand and brought it to his lips kissing the back. His eyes never left her face and she was feeling warm all over.

"What are you doing?" she said, trying to slow her rapidly beating heart down. "I thought you wanted that one."

"No, this one's fine," he said, looking at the jar she'd previously placed in the trolley.

"Are you sure? I don't mind." Her brows knitted together.

"Yes. It's your apartment and you like this. I don't want to change your shopping habits since I'm only at your place for the week."

She swayed and he quickly held her to him.

"Are you okay? I should have realised this was too much too fast," he said, concerned she wasn't up to even doing the grocery shopping.

"I-I'm fine. Let's just keep going," she said.

It was the fact Boston only saw himself staying for the week which threw her. She stupidly hoped perhaps this week could be a trial. See how they did as a couple being around each other constantly and they then could perhaps... she let the thought go.

Boston frowned, but did as Alyssa asked and continued to push the trolley all the while making sure he kept a close eye on her. He was enjoying spending time doing something so mundane with her and had completely forgotten she had even been in hospital. Seeing her sway was a frightful reminder that she was meant to be taking it easy.

By the time they headed to the checkout, she realised she forgot milk and ice cream.

"Oh shoot. I was supposed to get milk and ice cream," she said.

"Why don't I run and grab it. What kind of ice cream do you want?" he said.

"No, it's quicker if I go. You start unloading the trolley," she said.

"Okay."

She quickly rushed off and grabbed the milk and two tubs of ice cream, one chocolate chunk and the other caramel swirl. Coming back, she hoped she hadn't been too long only to come to a sudden stop as she saw a tall, lithe, blonde woman flirting with Boston. The woman who was ahead of him, was leaning over past him ensuring she collided with him to reach a packet of gum.

Anger swiftly rose as Alyssa watched how Boston hadn't even bothered to attempt to move back to give the lady room so she couldn't brush up against him.

The woman held up the gum for him to see and gave him a sly smile as he continued emptying their trolley.

Alyssa was furious. He was flirting with some other woman just because she wasn't around.

Looking up he saw her standing there and smiled.

"Great, you got it. I tried to go slow and hoped you wouldn't be too long," he said, as if nothing out the ordinary had just happened.

"Yes," she said, shaking her jealousy away until the

woman in front of them said with a saucy wink, "You've got my number. Call me."

Fury flashed across Alyssa's face, but she said nothing even though she was now spoiling for a fight. Snatching up one of the bags before Boston could do it, she stormed to the car wishing she could leave him at the store.

It wasn't until they got back to her apartment and she finished slamming the fridge and freezer doors that she finally erupted.

"I want you to leave. Right now," she said.

"What? Why?" he said, bemused.

"Why? You have to ask me, why?" Her voice rose to nearly shouting.

"Clearly, because I don't know what's gotten into you? Is your head troubling you?" he said.

She scowled at him. Typical to make it sound like she — not him — was the problem, she fumed to herself.

"I *saw* you." She jabbed her finger at him. "That's right. I saw you flirting with that woman. Is that what you do? I turn my back for two minutes and you're already chatting up another woman."

He looked stunned by the accusation.

"I wasn't flirting with her. I swear," he said.

"You need to leave," she said.

"I'm not leaving. I haven't done anything wrong. I swear I didn't hit on her. She flirted with me, but I never encouraged her."

"*Right*." She crossed her arms. "And I suppose I misheard her when she said for you to call her, that you had her number."

"Angel, there's no number. I swear. She was just causing trouble."

"Don't call me that. I'm *not* your angel," she hissed, not knowing what to believe. Her head was beginning to throb, which didn't help matters. "Why? Why would a complete stranger do that? It makes no sense unless you encouraged her. If you really didn't have her number then she'd get nothing out of it." She exhaled a loud breath and in a quiet tone said, "Please just leave."

Boston saw Alyssa's shoulders slump. He realised she was not only exhausted, but also feeling defeated. No one ever questioned his integrity because people knew he played straight as an arrow. He wasn't a liar and then instantly kicked himself as that was exactly what he was doing.

"I tell you what, you look exhausted. Why don't you go have a lie down and I'll put the rest of the groceries away. After you've rested, we'll talk, calmly. I swear I wasn't flirting. I wouldn't do that to you, Ang-Lys," he said, quickly stopping himself from calling her angel again since she didn't like that nickname either. But to him, Alyssa was his angel.

It was Boston's contrite tone which made Alyssa want to believe him and also made her want to cry. Nodding, she went to her bedroom to lie down, but first she had a little cry before she fell asleep.

Boston used the time Alyssa was resting to plan his attack. He knew the women at the store were flirting, yet to be malicious and say something which could ruin his already fragile relationship with Alyssa made him angry. He didn't know how he was supposed to convince her he really was innocent. It wasn't his style to be with one woman and then flirt or encourage others.

In the past, any woman who had shown this kind of possessiveness or jealousy, he would have just dumped. But this was Alyssa. His dream girl. He couldn't even take heart in the fact she was acting possessive or jealous because she wasn't. She was scared and frightened.

Then a great idea came to him. That's what they needed to do. They needed to use this week getting to know each other. Whatever it took, he'd do it and keep his hands to himself until he earned her trust. It didn't mean he wasn't allowed to steal kisses and hold her hand, but he wasn't about to seduce her into bed until she was sure of him or them. Then he instantly groaned to himself. His willpower was about to be tested beyond all reasonable limits. Nevertheless, Alyssa was worth it.

After she woke, Alyssa was feeling better and less emotional. Perhaps she overreacted to the women in the store. Deciding Boston was right and they needed to clear the air, she went into the lounge to see him hard at work.

"Hey, you're awake. How are you feeling?" he said, wary she might still be angry at him.

"Better," she sighed. "Do you promise you didn't flirt

with that woman in any way?"

"Promise," he said, sincere. "In fact, while you were asleep I thought about it and came up with an idea I hope you'll like."

"What's that?" she said.

"How about we use this week to get to know each other better. *And* I promise I won't even try to get you into bed. I'll be a true gentleman, although I would like your permission so we can still at least kiss, but *no sex* unless you say," he said.

She gave him a wary look, but liked the idea.

"You're not going to try and seduce me, to make me change my mind?" she said.

"I'll admit it'll be hard, but if I cross a line you don't like, you can send me packing. How's that?"

"I guess it sounds reasonable."

Thanks to their newfound agreement, Alyssa was feeling a lot more in control and the rest of the day was calm. She found Boston was funny and knowledgeable about so many things and although she really wanted to give him a passionate kiss goodnight, she didn't want to give him the wrong idea and left it as a simple goodnight before going to her room to his dismay.

Chapter Eight

After their initial rocky start to the week they began to find a rhythm. It didn't help that Alyssa was still recovering and so this wasn't a normal week in her life. There was only so much TV she could watch and magazines to read while Boston worked and after the first day, she really was going stir crazy. She was going to have to find some excuses to go out to the shops or just find something to do.

Boston had also decided that this week would be the perfect time to see if he could make the first step towards a better work/life balance. He was a renown workaholic because he was not only trying to build up his company, but also didn't want to lose the faith and trust his two brothers-in-law placed in him, as it was their money which helped him get his company off the ground.

Knowing he was luckier than most people to have such wonderful, supportive and *wealthy* relations, Boston wasn't about to take it for granted. However, now he had met Alyssa, things had changed. He knew he wanted both a happy family life and a successful company, just like his brothers-in-law and therefore needed to work on being a better CEO. Learning to trust his staff to handle the day to day operations whether he was there or not.

He also needed to learn how to be a better boyfriend since he could admit in all his previous relationships, he had been the selfish one, always putting work first unless it was an important occasion or event he needed to be present for. Most of his girlfriends understood this and at first never minded his workaholic ways after all, being the girlfriend of Boston Chan gave them attention and prestige. Then it would start getting tiresome that he was constantly working and never really relaxed.

Deciding he would work if Alyssa was resting or at night, but she would have his full attention when she was up and about. This was going to be a huge change for him and he wasn't sure if he could handle being spontaneous and going with the flow. His days were generally organised into time slots so he knew exactly where and what he was doing.

One morning Alyssa found Boston asleep on the couch and instantly felt guilty. He must have been so exhausted to have just fallen asleep there. Trying to be as quiet as she could, she made simple egg omelettes and toast for breakfast to show her appreciation at his sacrifice and she was thankful to have him around.

The thought then gave her cause to frown again. How come she couldn't remember him? Not even a tiny little flicker of memory. That was the part which deep down made her anxious. Was there something about Boston which was why her memory refused to acknowledge his existence? Deciding if her memory of Boston didn't return by the time Uncle Jack returned from his trip, she'd get him to dig into Boston's background for her. It seemed underhanded and deceitful, however it might be the only way to shed some light on who Boston Chan really was.

Boston woke to a delicious smell and as he scrubbed his face, gave a big yawn. He had slept the entire night on the couch in his clothes. Looking over and seeing Alyssa brightly smiling at him as she placed two plates onto the table, he couldn't help but feel happy.

"You're awake," she said. "Just in time for breakfast. I wasn't too sure if I should wake you or not, but since you now are, come and eat."

"I definitely can't turn down a delicious smelling meal. You didn't have to make me breakfast, toast would have been fine."

Yes, it was definitely happiness he felt especially seeing how Alyssa had made an effort for him. His breakfast was usually toast, which didn't bother him. It was that or muesli with yoghurt and fruit to make him feel like he was at least eating something healthy, especially since he had a lot of business lunches and dinners.

"Oh crap," he said, suddenly remembering an appointment.

"What?"

"I forgot, I've got an important meeting at one-thirty today I need to be in the office for. Don't worry, I'll reschedule."

"Don't be silly. I'll be fine here by myself," she said, feeling guilty.

It wasn't like Boston to have forgotten something so important but then, everything was out of kilter for him at the moment.

"No, I'll just move it online," he said, knowing Mr Yamaguchi wouldn't be very happy. The man preferred dealing with people face to face, which was one of the reasons Boston liked him, because he preferred to do the same.

"Then I'll come with you," she said.

"Huh?"

She almost giggled at his confusion.

"Well, I'm feeling a little housebound so it would be nice to get out for a bit. How long's your meeting? I could always come with you and walk around the shops and get a change of scenery," she said.

He almost sagged in relief. Alyssa's suggestion made him not only feel more comfortable, but would also help solve his problem.

"Are you sure you're up to it? I don't want you over

exerting yourself."

She not only could hear the hope, but also the relief in Boston's voice.

"I'll stay close to your work and if I'm feeling tired, I'll just come back to your office and wait for you."

He looked torn.

"I guess the meeting is only supposed to be an hour. You'll have your phone on you, right?" he said.

"Of course."

"Okay then, we'll go into work. You can walk around as long as you promise if you're not feeling up to it, you'll come back to the office to rest," he said. "I'll have my secretary make sure there's somewhere quiet you can lie down if you need to. And you'll have your phone on you."

"Good grief, you sound like my Uncle Jack," she said.

"Not your father?"

It was an innocent enough question, but for Alyssa she was just now realising she didn't have any memories of a father. The only father in her mind was Uncle Jack so what happened to her real one? Had he died or was it something else?

"Are you okay?" he said, concerned she looked pale.

"F-fine. Just need a minute that's all."

"Did you remember your father?" he said, hesitant.

"No."

Not wanting to start an argument about Alyssa's father and their relationship, Boston let his curiosity slide hoping Alyssa would eventually open up to him about it, if she wanted.

"Okay. Give me your phone and I'll programme my number in and vice versa," he said.

"You don't already have it?" Now she was confused. Why would she not have Boston's phone number already nor he, hers?

Seeing his mistake, he quickly thought of a logical explanation and went with the near truth. Taking a deep breath, he confessed.

"I'll be honest. We only just met before you had your accident and we really hadn't —"

"What?" she shrieked. "I thought we had been dating for a while. That's what you led me to believe and now you say you've been lying this whole time? Had I known I'd only just met you, then there's no way I'd have let you stay here."

"I know," he said, hoping to calm her down. "I'm sorry, but when the hospital rang and you didn't have anyone else to help you —"

"And it's *rather convenient* I don't remember you," she said, irate.

He raked a hand through his hair, knowing this wasn't going any way he wanted it to and began to worry.

"I really am sorry. I really did want to help you."

"You could be an axe murderer or some kind of con man for all I know," she said.

"What do you want to do? I'll leave if you really want. You seem to be better or at least enough so I don't need to watch over you," he said, hoping and praying she'd still give him a chance even if she did kick him out.

Now Alyssa was torn. Finding out she didn't really know Boston explained why she didn't have the memories she thought she was missing. On the other hand, what if he truly was a con man and knew just how to manipulate her?

Unsure what to do, she wondered if she could get Uncle Jack to return to New York earlier and then sighed, realising it was being a bit dramatic. She wasn't hurt and was old enough to know her own mind, wasn't she? Was knowing your own mind a thing when you don't have your entire memory back? What if she did get it all back and realised she didn't like Boston at all from their initial encounter? Somehow she couldn't imagine it but still, it was a possibility.

Or maybe this was the chance she needed to actually get to know him. What if she thought at the time she met him he wasn't her type, but now after getting to know him, she saw him in a different light, something which might never have happened if it hadn't been for her accident.

In all honesty, she was attracted to Boston and could only pray this wasn't going to end up being a horrendous mistake on her part.

"Why don't we just go into your office, you have your meeting, I'll go for a walk and then we can sort this out after," she sighed, knowing it sounded very wishy-washy and undecisive, but she still didn't know what to do. Perhaps a walk in the fresh air would help her process her thoughts better.

"Okay," he said, relieved she hadn't just immediately kicked him out.

Once they arrived at his office building and they got out of the elevator on the ground floor, he said, "Are you sure you don't want to come up to the office first?"

"No, I think I'll just walk."

"I'm on the fifty-first floor. I'll let reception know you might pop in and they'll send you down to my office where you can wait."

"Okay." She nodded, then checked her watch. "I'll see you in a couple of hours."

"Unless I call you to let you know I've finished early."

"Or, I'll just be waiting in the lobby and you can do some other work if I'm early and don't want to come up."

"Okay, we'll keep in touch with each other. I'll text when my meeting's finished and you can let me know what you want to do," he said.

"Okay."

It was an awkward goodbye, almost as if they were just acquaintances rather than in a fledging relationship since there was no kissing, hugging or any kind of touching. As they both went their separate ways, Boston wanted to chase after her, yet made himself keep walking into the elevator.

He needed to get his mind focused and on his meeting.

Mr Yamaguchi was a wily businessman, another reason Boston liked him but still, he wasn't about to let the older man out negotiate him just because his mind was on Alyssa and not the deal.

Alyssa was relieved to be outside and by herself. She already felt better at the change of scenery and knew this had been the right decision even if her mind constantly whirled with thoughts about Boston.

Perhaps she should go up to his office early just to see what he did or talk to someone there, just to ask some general questions about him. It would ease her mind, but then part of her didn't want to know more about him. Part of her wanted to bury her head in the sand because she was worried if he truly wasn't the real deal then she'd be more than upset. There was just something about Boston which drew her to him. She felt a connection and the thought this was all a sham on his part would be devastating. But wouldn't it be better to know now before he could con her even more?

Round and round the questions and denial went in her mind, almost driving her crazy and before she knew it, she was back at the start in the building lobby still debating whether she should go up to Boston's office or not.

Before she could make a firm decision, she saw Boston walking towards her with the biggest smile on his face. This was the reason she didn't want to know if he was conning her. He was looking at her like she was his everything and she liked that feeling a lot.

"How was your walk?" He marvelled at how much he wanted her near him all the time, that even a few hours apart was too long.

"Good. How was your meeting?" she said.

"It went well, although Mr Yamaguchi is a wily old fox," he chuckled.

Alyssa heard the respect in Boston's voice for the man and smiled.

"Is he a client?" she said.

"No, he's just someone who I sometimes do business with to our mutual benefit. I have a lot of respect for him."

"Well, I'm sure he feels the same for you."

Alyssa's compliment warmed him.

"I'm not sure about that. He's trying to offload one of his poorly performing companies onto me for a premium," he chuckled.

"So he thinks you're an easy target?" she said, confused.

"Yes and no. He likes a good haggle and knows I don't really want it. However, while that may be the case, I do know someone who would be interested, so we'll play cat and mouse, trying to out manoeuvre the other," he said. "I'll probably end up buying it like he wants and then flick it off to the other person who wants it."

"Why don't you just give him the name of the other person and they can do a deal?" she said.

"What and lose out on my cut? I'm not letting him know that I know someone who wants it," he laughed.

Alyssa just sighed, then smiled at how complicated the business world could be. Her Uncle Jack was much the same. It seemed all men seemed to view this as fun and sport.

Although the rest of their day went well and they had dinner at a lovely little restaurant she liked, she was now having a hard time sleeping. Deciding to get a drink, she quietly went upstairs to the kitchen only to be surprised to see Boston sitting at the table working.

"Oh. Here I am creeping around and you're still working," she said, embarrassed.

She could see his hungry eyes devouring her in his mind, making her feel hot and bothered.

Boston never imagined seeing a woman in a plain cotton nightshirt would be so sexy. It was the buttons, he decided. The chance to open one button at a time to reveal his fantasy, which was now making him aroused.

It was one of the reasons he was still up working. The place was quiet and it took his mind off Alyssa in bed where he hoped she was naked and preferably waiting for him. Now he knew the truth, it didn't make his arousal wane in the slightest, it just ramped it up.

"What are you doing up?" he said, wondering if he should start unbuttoning her nightshirt from the bottom or the top or even better, alternating. Then he'd get the pleasure of revealing her silky-smooth legs and the teasing of her breasts at the same time.

"Couldn't sleep. Thought a drink of water would help," she said.

"You know, there's a well-documented cure for aiding sleep," he grinned.

"Hot milk, I know, but I can't be bothered," she sighed, and it took him a minute to realise she was serious and he almost laughed to himself.

"Why are you still working?" she said, curious.

He didn't want to admit he found her too distracting but then again, maybe if he was honest then perhaps she might take pity on him and finally let him into her bed.

"You're too distracting during the day and therefore I don't get enough work done. Don't worry, I'm used to working long into the night. If you must know, I'm a workaholic," he said.

"Really?" she said, surprised before frowning. "I don't think you are, or at least no more so than some people I know."

"That's because I'm working now long after you've gone to bed so you don't see," he smiled.

"Don't you ever have any down time?"

It was such an innocent question and he was feeling very devilish.

"Of course, but usually it's only when I have a *bed buddy*."

"Is that some kind of book/tablet thing?" she said, puzzled.

"No." Surely she couldn't be *that* naive.

She frowned before realising exactly what he meant.

"Oh," she blushed.

He couldn't stop himself from grinning. Alyssa really was temptation, which made him sigh.

"I won't keep you from your work," she said, getting her drink and then going back to her room.

Yes, it was going to be another *long, cold* shower again tonight, he groaned to himself.

Chapter Nine

The next day, Boston told Alyssa that he had some urgent stuff he needed to get done.

"That's fine. I can go out by myself and leave you in peace," she said.

"No," he said, a little too abrupt. "I mean, I want to spend time with you, but I really need to do this. Do you mind waiting for a couple of hours?"

"Won't I be annoying you?"

"Not really. I mean, I won't be concentrating on work as much as I normally would if I was at the office, but I'll still get it done. It'll be good for me to know that you're waiting and I have to finish otherwise I'll just keep going," he said.

The thought warmed her that Boston was using her as a reason to take a break.

"Okay, I'll just watch some TV."

Alyssa couldn't help but note Boston seemed to be churning through quite a bit with intensity and a laser focus. Clearly this was how he got to be so successful.

Then her thoughts turned to wondering if he wanted a wife and family in the future. If he did, would he cut back on work for them? This then led to wondering what she did or didn't know about him in a personal capacity.

"I can hear your brain churning from over here," he smiled, looking up from his laptop.

His comment made her flush as she thought he was too focused on his work to sense her deep in thought.

"I was just wondering what…" She wasn't sure how to say what she wanted to say without feeling embarrassed.

"What?"

"What do I know about you as a person." She grimaced at how ridiculous she sounded.

He grinned and her stomach fluttered like every other time he smiled at her.

"What would you like to know?"

"Everything?"

"That's a bit broad," he chuckled. "Tell you what, it's a nice day. Why don't we go for a walk and talk, then have some lunch out somewhere."

"That sounds perfect. It would be nice to get out of the house."

Seeing the happiness on her face made him feel guilty

while he had things to occupy him, she didn't.

"Give me another hour to wrap this up and then we'll head out."

It turned out to be an hour and a half later because Jason called to let him know Indi had given birth to a little boy, and between the excitement of this news, Boston also managed a quick catch up on family news knowing all his siblings were sure to be ringing each other to catch up and share in the excitement.

Now they were walking around the park, Alyssa felt brave enough to bring up his telephone conversation.

"I don't mean to be nosy, but you seemed very excited on your phone call. Good news?" she said.

"Yes, my sister has just given birth to my new nephew."

"Oh, that's fantastic. Is it her first?"

Boston thought it was nice Alyssa seemed just as excited as he was.

"No, her second and knowing her, probably not the last either. She's so in love with her hubby I reckon they'll have at least four," he chuckled.

"Oh wow," she said, "I didn't realise you had siblings. How many? Is it just your sister?"

As they walked, he smiled to himself at Alyssa's question. This was the part of meeting someone he got to enjoy when he explained his family. All his siblings enjoyed telling people not only how many of them there were, but also their names as it always gave them a good laugh at people's reactions.

"Actually I'm one of six," he said.

"Six?" Her eyes boggled and then she looked wistful. "Oh, I'm so jealous. I wish I had one sibling let alone six? Are they all sisters? Brothers? What?"

He smiled at her inquisitiveness.

"Four sisters and one brother. My brother and I consider ourselves buffers between the warring factions that are my sisters. Two are older and bossy and the other two are younger and brats."

Hearing the love in his voice for his siblings, Alyssa sighed. It must have been great growing up in a family like that. The fighting and squabbling, but also all the fun times they probably had.

"You're so lucky. Being an only child is no picnic," she said.

"It's never boring, that's for sure," he said. "Even now there's always someone in your business whether you like it or not."

Boston was a typical middle child although technically, he and his younger brother Phoenix were the middle children however he wasn't as rowdy as his sibling. He was also the quieter more thoughtful one of the family.

All his sisters did was constantly talk with whispers, giggles, screeching and shouting, whether it was with or at each other, depending on what day or time it was. It invariably always ended up with the two eldest sisters ganging up on the two younger ones and them fighting back because they didn't like being bossed about.

In their younger years he had tried to play peace-maker and learnt his lesson well. Don't get involved in his sisters' arguments because they'll turn on you instead.

The first time it happened, his head was left spinning for days after the girls were fighting over being dropped off to their respective locales.

Being neutral, Boston interceded with reasonable logic thinking to solve all their problems, which would make his sisters happy. Unfortunately, he completely misunderstood their desire to not want logic to interfere with their arguments, especially at their ages.

His sisters may have remained quiet as he explained his solution however, by the time he finished and was feeling quite the satisfied mediator, in a blink of an eye they all turned on him with yelling and shouting about his unwanted and unneeded interference into their argument. By the time they had finished scolding him, somewhere, somehow, they were now all friends again having fought the common enemy and Boston was a bewildered mess.

Another time his older sister, Indi had dragged him into the argument as the deciding vote. Both sides argued and when he picked the younger sisters' idea over his older sisters all hell broke loose, with Montana and Indi both becoming angry with him.

Having learnt from that lesson, the next time he was dragged into an argument, he put forth another neutral rational solution only to be furiously beaten down again.

It was then it dawned on him that he was never going to win and sisters were complicated with a capital C.

Luckily after his epiphany he and his younger brother, Phoenix would either hide if a fight was occurring or quickly depart so they couldn't be pulled into the middle of it. Sometimes just to mess with them, the brothers would purposefully each take a side so it made the girls keep arguing. Not only did it let them off the hook, their sisters moaned at how stupid the brother who didn't take their side was or how the brother who took their side was the smarter one.

Boston smiled at the thought of being one of six children. Not only that, but their names were all so unique that people always were amazed their parents could name them so distinctively.

Now he could see the advantages to having a big family and one with unique names, but in his childhood it was horrible as there was no such thing as privacy and the teasing over their names was almost a daily occurrence.

Although Boston was the third born, he was also the eldest son and as such felt it was his duty to look after his siblings along with Montana who was the eldest. It was a job he took seriously and was the protective brother who drove all his sisters crazy judging by the constant complaints to their parents about him interfering in their lives.

His youngest sisters had the most to moan about, which didn't stop him from giving any boy who came near his sisters a look that said, *you're too close and get at least ten feet back.*

Thomas Chan would just smile as his wife tried to calm the girls down. They were proud of all their children however, Thomas could see Boston was not only a good son, but also a good brother no matter how much his siblings hated his interference. He also didn't worry about his children if Boston was with them because he knew his eldest son was very responsible and would never let anything happen to his siblings.

Where girls seemed to be drawn to Phoenix's extrovert, arrogant and fiery personality like moths to a flame, Boston was quieter and more serious and therefore wasn't as interested in a revolving door of girlfriends to sow his wild oats. It didn't mean he was a monk. He just wasn't a prolific serial dater like some of the guys he knew. He was marriage or serious boyfriend material and as much as women said that's what they wanted, ironically they were the ones who didn't when he wanted to take a more serious step in their relationship.

Always one to be rational and logical about situations, it was what made people trust him and even many of his ex-girlfriends were still friends with him. This reasoning explained why he had never told anyone apart from his family that he loved them.

They weren't words he chose to bandy about like some people. To him he would only say it if he really truly meant it and thus far, he hadn't met that person. Although Alyssa was fast changing that.

Since he was so close to his siblings, he found girlfriends would get annoyed and were even slightly jealous he was always taking calls from his family, especially his sisters. Even his male friends would tease him about the fact that he talked regularly to his sisters. Thus he began calling them sunshine, doll face and any number of generic nicknames, which earned him loads of grief from his sisters about how he didn't use their names if he was with friends. This in turn led to them trying to provoke Boston into making him say either their names or something mushy like, 'I love you', just for a laugh and of course to try and embarrass him. It was times like this he loved having so many siblings until they made him want to tear his hair out again.

"So which sister had the baby?" Alyssa said.

"My second eldest sister, Indiana. She lives in England with her *hunky* husband," he said, making her laugh.

"Sounds wonderful and romantic." She sighed once again. "Wait," she said, as if an epiphany struck. "Your sister's name is Indiana and you're Boston, what are the rest of your siblings' names?"

"Want to guess? I'll give you a clue. We were all named after places in America. The eldest two were named after States. My brother and I are named after State capitals and the brats, well…" He grinned and shrugged, as if their names weren't important at all like them.

Alyssa began throwing out all the names of places she could think of, hoping to just hit one by fluke.

"Let's see… Houston, Dallas, Virginia, Dakota, Ohio, Chicago, Orlando, Miami, Portland, Missouri, Oregon, New York, New Jersey. Am I getting close?"

"Not really," he smiled. "My brother's the easiest. He's a city in Arizona."

"Phoenix!" Her face lit up at the answer and he couldn't help but laugh.

"You got it."

"My other older sister is a State up north bordering Canada, surrounded by Idaho, the Dakotas and Wyoming."

"I have no idea. What does it start with?" she said, looking deep in thought.

"M."

"M… M… M…" she said, over and over before shaking her head. "Michigan and Maine are the only two I can think of off the stop of my head."

"Starts with M, is seven letters and ends in A."

"Montana!" she squealed, delighted.

"There you go," he laughed, enjoying seeing the happiness on her face.

"I think you're just going to have to tell me the last two names. I don't think I have the brain power to work it out. My mind just goes blank and not because I can't remember either."

The way she was smiling and joking, Boston realised coming out today and talking about his siblings was a great idea. It had made Alyssa feel normal and forget her memory loss for a little while.

"Alexandria or as we call her, Lexi because she hates Alex. Of course, we all call her that when we want to annoy her, which sometimes can be quite often," he chuckled. "And the baby of the family is Savannah."

"Oh, I love those names" she gushed. "My name just seems so boring in comparison."

"It's perfect, just like you."

The heat in his eyes made her blush.

"Come on, let's go eat. I don't know about you, but I'm starving," he said.

She giggled and happily put her arm around his waist to hold him closer and Boston couldn't help but smile.

Chapter Ten

Although the day was great talking and sharing stories, Alyssa couldn't help but find herself fascinated with Boston's family. What it must be like to be one of six siblings, she enviously sighed to herself.

"What's that sigh for?" he said, kissing the top of her head as they sat on the couch not really watching the TV.

"I'm just so jealous you have so many siblings. The stories you have to tell, whether they're funny, embarrassing, just plain crazy and loving. It just makes me sad I have none of those."

He held her closer to him, kissing her head once again.

"The stories about you and your friends are pretty similar. Of course, you didn't have a ton of door slamming from your sisters. Your homelife was nice and serene, not a constant battleground like mine."

"That's true," she sighed. "Still, it would have been nice to have at least one sibling to fight with."

"Would you rather have a brother or sister. Believe me, each come with their own set of pros and cons."

"Really? Tell me," she said, eager to hear more.

"Well, Nix was the family hothead growing up and the jump in and ask questions later kind of guy. Although it always came from a good place with good intentions, having to stop him from getting into scraps or getting him out of them was exhausting. Thankfully, he's a lot better now, I guess time and maturity has mellowed him, a little," he chuckled. "Then the sisters, where do I start? Older is bossier and younger is just a pain in the you-know-what, but I love my sisters and have to say we're definitely a lot closer now that we're adults. I guess it's because we've stopped tormenting each other so much. Well, unless we're all together then it's a free for all."

"Can you tell me some stories about you and your siblings growing up?" she said, eager to hear how wonderful it must have been to have siblings.

He gave it a moment's thought.

"One of our best stories is what we like to call The Great Strawberry War of 1818," he laughed.

"That's sounds like so much fun. Tell me."

"One day our parents told us we were going to spend the day at our Uncle Doug's strawberry farm, which to us sounded like Christmas with thoughts of stuffing our faces with tons of strawberries until we were sick. Those thoughts were quickly dashed when we were told we were actually being drafted in to help pick the berries."

"Oh no," she groaned, thinking it now sounded like everyone's nightmare.

"The upshot was that after being in the hot sun and finally finishing for the day, we were all cranky and tired. However, we were allowed to eat any of the 'unsellable' ones and while we enjoyed eating the fruits of our labour…"

Alyssa laughed at the pun as Boston smiled.

"Lexi, although she'll deny it until her dying day, started the war by hitting Indi with one of her strawberry tops and before we all knew it, we were all just throwing strawberries at each other." He laughed at the memory.

"Didn't you get into trouble?" she gasped, before giggling.

"Yes, but it was so much fun that we didn't care and to be honest, I think our parents didn't actually mind since they knew how hard we had worked."

"Wow, makes me wish I had siblings for those kinds of memories."

"Then there was the time Indi accidentally kissed the wrong guy. Now that was hilarious," he chuckled.

Alyssa sat there gobsmacked torn between laughter and shock.

"I know. You're thinking how do you kiss the wrong guy?"

She nodded.

"It turns out that she saw him from afar, thought he was her boyfriend and went over to surprise him. She tapped him on the shoulder and when he turned, she kissed him. That was fine until they stopped and she realised the guy she was kissing was someone completely different."

Now Alyssa felt embarrassed for Boston's sister.

"What made it worse was the guy thought it was great until his girlfriend came over furious, so my sister quickly scarpered," he said.

"Oh no, she must have been so embarrassed. How did she get it so wrong?" she said.

"She was, and I only know because I overheard my sisters talking about it. Turns out that she wasn't wearing her glasses to see that far away properly so the guy was slightly blurry, which was why she made the mistake." Boston laughed.

"Oh dear. I wonder if that guy and girl are still together," she giggled.

"Who knows but FYI, I told my brother and let's just say we ensured that she was even more mortified and to this day, we both still like to tease her about putting her glasses on."

Boston's stories made Alyssa envious. Sure, she had stories like that about her friends, but what would it have been like to actually have siblings to constantly tease you about your mistakes or embarrassing moments in life. To know how much you love each other.

Alyssa sat there cuddling Boston and realised that was the kind of life she wanted. A home and loving family, squabbling children.

Seeing Alyssa with a thoughtful look on her face, Boston was anxious about what she was thinking.

"What are you thinking?"

"I want you," she whispered.

Boston froze unsure if he heard her correctly. His eyes searched her face as she smiled, the look in her eyes showing her desire. That was all he needed as his mouth found hers.

If he had known spending time talking about themselves would end up with her inviting him into her bed, he would have done it on day one. Kissing Alyssa was spectacular. The connection was more powerful than he'd ever experienced, just as somewhere deep in the recesses of his mind, he knew it would be. From the moment he saw her, there was an undeniable connection between them.

"Make love to me," she whispered.

"Are you sure?" He was only asking because he knew once they started he didn't want to stop.

"Yes, I'm sure."

As soon as they were in her room, his hand threaded into her silky hair and anchored her head while his mouth plundered hers.

Alyssa felt stuck between falling off a cliff and holding on for dear life.

It was a slightly frenzied event, but she didn't want slow and sedate. She wanted Boston badly. Her whole body shaking with desire.

Boston was trying to slow down and make their first time memorable, but Alyssa turned him on like an out of control wildfire. Somehow clothes managed to be shed and limbs untangled for the briefest of moments.

He rose up to look at her naked and ready for him. She was gorgeous. All her satiny skin on display made him want to taste her everywhere and she wasn't shy either as she openly ogled his well-toned body with the same look of lust as she licked her lips.

"L-Lys," he rasped, as he began to taste her, up dale and down valley over her breasts making her pant. His deft fingers lightly glided down her body and along her thighs. She parted her legs so he could feel her slickness of sexual desire for him.

Placing himself over her, there wasn't a coherent thought left as he entered her swiftly making her gasp at the sheer size of him.

He took her mouth and then moved with deliberate strokes, teasing her until he felt her begin to tense and then climax.

Alyssa writhed under Boston, raising her hips, needing him deeper and urging him to go faster. His teasing didn't just frustrate her, it excited her so much she felt herself explode.

Crying out his name as she scored his back with her

fingers pierced his lust-filled mind as he couldn't stop himself from following.

They lay there sated for now and Boston felt guilty he hadn't taken more time to worship Alyssa, but instead took her with the lust of a hormonal teenage boy.

"I think I've proven my point, don't you? You can't fit in this bed," she giggled, recalling their argument when she first returned home as a deep growl came from the back of his throat making her shiver.

"But I fit perfectly somewhere else," he said, moving to kiss her thoroughly before moving down her neck to her breasts and grazing her nipples with his teeth making her breath catch and soon she was soaring to the stars yet again.

"You need a bigger bed," he groaned, as they were a tangle of arms and legs.

"But I like my bed," she said. "It's *very* comfy."

His eyes flashed and this time she knew what was going to happen and was excited. She wanted and needed him.

Alyssa moaned at what Boston was doing. She was lucky to have a boyfriend who knew how to turn her into a blazing inferno was her last coherent thought for the rest of the night.

Later, as she cuddled him, Boston felt a sense of peace come over him. He had expected fantastic sex and with Alyssa in his arms he was now happily and contently enjoying the quiet. She was a marvel. God knows she had him tied up in knots since the hospital, but his angel blew any and all expectations out of the water. Their connection seemed more spectacular than with anyone he had ever known. Was this how his sisters felt with their husbands?

The next morning Alyssa woke and realised Boston had indeed managed to spend the night in her bed, albeit with him being at slightly awkward angles so he could fit. She wondered if he was going to complain about all the kinks and knots he was bound to have.

She couldn't get out of the bed without having to move him and so she lay there thinking about last night and what an amazing lover he was. Automatically she stretched herself like a cat forgetting she could wake him.

Realising he was now awake as his hand moved up her stomach to her breast, she couldn't help but smile as she turned her head to look at him and through sleepy eyes he smiled.

"Good morning. So what will it be?" he said, enjoying waking up next to Alyssa. Nothing had felt more right.

She looked at him blankly, unsure what he was talking about, yet even if she did know, the circular patterns his finger was making were distracting her from thinking.

"New bed or my place?"

"How about I see *your* place, check out *your* bed and then decide." She gave him a seductive smile.

"You're a saucy vixen. If you keep that up, we won't be going anywhere."

"In that case I'd better get up and ready to go," she teased.

He held her tightly to him and she felt his morning arousal, which in turn made her aroused.

"I'm already up and ready to go," he grinned.

She laughed as he began making love to her once again.

Reluctantly they left her bed and went to his place. Upon entering his luxurious apartment, Alyssa was despondent she felt nothing, not a single tingle or even memory. She had been apprehensive on the drive over and even in the elevator felt like she didn't know which way to jump. Boston held her hand and as he opened the door, she held her breath. Everything all looked blank to her and she was scared. How could she not remember him, yet she could remember work?

"Are you okay?" he said, concerned.

"Yes. I just can't understand why I don't remember you or this place. Not even a little bit,' she said, blinking back the tears starting to form.

"Well, I think that's made the decision easier. New bed it is," he said, with a gentle teasing smile and ignoring his guilt over the fact that she had never been here.

"Well, while we're here we really should test out your bed for research purposes. After all, size and firmness does matter."

Her blatant come-on even though she was upset aroused him. There were many times he spent non-stop weekends in bed with women, but after each coupling the desire lessened until it burnt out. Alyssa wasn't like that. She made him crave her more, like an addiction.

Once again he dampened the little flicker of guilt in which she was trying hard to remember something that was never there to begin with. Scooping her up, he carried her to his bed so they could begin their research.

"Does it feel like the first time for you too or was it always like this?" she said, when they were back at her place.

He knew exactly what she was asking and needed to tread carefully so he didn't spook her or lie even more.

"Every time with you feels like the first time."

"That's a terribly cheesy response," she laughed.

"I'll be honest, what we have together is so extraordinary that I think what we feel is on a whole other level."

Although relieved and heartened by his answer since she too felt a connection with Boston, she was sure she had never experienced before, she still felt a little niggling sensation and it worried her.

He bought her a new bed and they made sure to thoroughly test it and with frequency. Alyssa knew that even if she couldn't remember Boston, she was now irrevocably in love with him.

The week they spent together was probably the happiest time in her life. They seemed to be comfortable in each other's presence which was reassuring. Sometimes Boston would pop into work for a while and she either went with him to walk around the shops or stayed home and pottered.

She even ventured into her work, happy she could remember everyone and everything. It made her feel normal somehow.

She also liked that Boston seemed interested in her enough to ask questions about her and her life, even if she either didn't feel comfortable or quite know the answer. Case in point, her father.

"Tell me what it was like growing up as an only child?" he said. "I mean, I'd think it was bliss. All that peace, no bickering with anyone. Able to do whatever you wanted, no babysitting. Although I guess I'd like at least one sibling."

"That's sort of how I feel. I mean, I know no different but one sibling would have been nice. My mother died of cancer when I was a teenager."

"I'm sorry, I hadn't realised," he said, holding her close, sensing she was still upset.

"It was horrible. That's why Uncle Jack entered the picture." She didn't mention the car incident.

"So, he's your mother's brother?"

"No, my father's."

As much as Boston didn't want to ask the question, he knew he had to.

"Where was your father?"

It was an odd question to have someone ask where a

person's father was when the uncle, the father's own brother, had been on the scene and Boston hoped that Alyssa hadn't lost two parents as that would be tragic.

"I'll be honest, I really don't remember. I remember everything about my mother, yet my father is a complete blank. I don't feel like he's dead or died, but for some reason I just don't remember him."

Now Boston felt terrible bringing up something that clearly wasn't so cut and dry for Alyssa.

"Tell me about your mum."

Listening to Alyssa wax lyrical about her mother showed just how much she loved and still missed her. She seemed to have the same kind of relationship his sisters had with their mother.

"So Uncle Jack is now more like a father to me or a really sleazy uncle that you either cringe or roll your eyes about. Thankfully, he's never acted that way around me or my friends growing up, but these days, ick," she said, screwing up her face and making him laugh.

Through it all as various bits and pieces of her memory came back, still none seemed to contain Boston. And even though he mentioned why that might be, the fact she didn't even have the memory of meeting him at all, just kept that niggling feeling constantly irritating her like a small pebble in your shoe you just can't find and get rid of. Thus she just kept driving herself crazy over whether Boston was a genuinely nice guy or a dirty rotten scoundrel.

Alyssa now felt ready to go back to work and with reality knocking on their door, both of them were quiet at dinner.

"So…" she said.

Boston had never felt so content, or had a relationship which wasn't just based on sex or his money. Alyssa delighted him all the time, but every now and then he'd see a faraway look in her eyes and dreaded the day when she looked at him with anger or hurt when she found out he had lied to her. Now he felt like the sword of Damocles was hanging over his head and about to drop.

"So," he said.

She was scared to bring up the big decision about their living arrangements and played with the food on her plate.

Boston, not one to shy away from the hard decisions did it for her.

"Do you want me to move out or you could move in with me?" It wasn't that he didn't like her place, but after a week the walls were closing in.

"Why don't we just see how it goes," she said, with a lack of enthusiasm. "I think I need to stay here while I get back to work. No offence, but your place is too…" She didn't finish, yet he understood. It was a blank in her mind and she didn't feel comfortable.

"Okay, well do you want me to stay?"

It would be so easy to say yes, but as the week went on, she noticed him chafing and being restless in her tiny home. Like he needed to get out or be somewhere with more space.

"No. I'll be fine now. Besides, I'll still see you all the time and we'll talk. Like you said, this is all very new for both of us so a little space could let us see if we're in it for the long haul."

"Fine," he said. "I'll pack up after dinner."

She wanted to cry and beg him to stay however, he seemed relieved to be getting away and she had some pride.

"Great," she mumbled.

After he packed, he went to reach out and touch her, but she turned pretending she hadn't realised his intentions and busily began tidying.

"Well, I guess I'll be off then."

The atmosphere in the room was heavy with neither of them really talking to the other.

"Okay." She stopped what she was doing and came over to him.

Their kiss seemed awkward, lacked passion and was so brief Alyssa could have imagined it.

"I'll call you," he said, cupping the side of her face.

"Sure." She quickly shut the door behind her and then promptly burst into tears.

Chapter Eleven

Alyssa was thankful work was a great distraction to worrying or even thinking about Boston. He called to wish her luck in the morning for her first day back and to call him if she needed anything.

Work hadn't been told about her memory loss and Alyssa felt that it wasn't really required since she remembered all the people there and her job. It was good to feel like she was back to normal even though she knew she wasn't.

"Hello, Alyssa speaking," she said, answering her phone.

"Hi Lys," Claire chirped. "Are you, and I hope your hot new boyfriend, free on Saturday night for games night?"

Alyssa panicked for a minute not knowing who was on the other end of the phone.

"Well…" She stalled, scrambling for a memory, but nothing happened.

"Don't tell me you and the hottie are so loved up that you don't want to socialise with us. Liz and I need some new eye candy to drool over too." Claire teased, oblivious to Alyssa's distress.

"Oh, well, you see," she said, but in the background she heard someone yelling the name Claire.

"The boss is having a tanty, so get back to me later. Love ya."

The call disconnected and her brain started to hurt as images of a woman with red hair laughing and smiling flooded her memory. Alyssa waited for the words to come, but then there was another woman with blonde hair. The three of them laughing in different scenarios, doing different things together.

She closed her eyes, holding her head in her hands as her heart raced with the speed of the mental images switching so fast. She knew they were her friends, Claire and Liz. Her hands were now shaking at the force of the memories returning and her head pounding with pain. Deciding she needed some fresh air, she quickly changed her mind and told her boss she needed to go home because of a headache.

Boston couldn't concentrate. He had left three messages for Alyssa and she had returned none. Short of going over to her work to demand a reason and looking like a bully, he very begrudgingly cooled his heels. He knew of women who would stop important meetings to take his calls, not that he was ever impressed, but being ignored by Alyssa was not a feeling he liked at all.

He called her later that night.

"Just wanted to see how your first day back was?" And to ask why you didn't return my calls, he thought.

"Busy. Tons of stuff to catch up on," she lied. She didn't want to admit to coming home early because of a headache because she knew Boston would not only have scolded her for trying to do too much too fast, but he would have also ended up at her place to keep an eye on her and right now she didn't want him hovering. She needed some breathing room.

Boston felt a little placated she wasn't ignoring him.

"That's good. Listen, I forgot to tell you that I'm away for the next few weeks, depending on how my trip goes. Will you be all right by yourself?" he said, concerned. He didn't want to leave her alone.

Alyssa could feel Boston pulling away from her and wasn't about to beg him for attention.

"Of course. Besides I've got other friends to catch up with."

The tone of her voice was chilly and Boston could tell Alyssa was annoyed with him. He had planned to go over and see her tonight, but with her demeanour at the moment, it was probably better to let her have some space.

Maybe after his trip they could get things back on track.

"Okay then. I'll see you when I get back."

Alyssa was mad at Boston. He didn't even want to see her before he left, which just went to show what kind of boyfriend he really was. A selfish one who had been saddled with her because no one else could do it and at the first chance of escape, he took it. She wondered if he even had a business trip, since he never mentioned one in all the time he stayed with her and he would have known about it.

Uncle Jack called the next day.

"Hi sunshine, how's things?" he said.

"I'm great. How's your trip?" At least her uncle cared.

"Fantastic. Your father sends his love."

Her father? Oh-oh. She still didn't remember her own father.

"Tell him I said hi the next time you talk to him," she said, not wanting to alarm him.

"Okay."

Phew, she thought. So her father wasn't here but lived overseas, which could explain why Alyssa didn't remember him. She did remember her mother and the photos around her place helped. There were none of anyone who could resemble a father figure except Uncle Jack. So who was her father? Knowing she must be on good terms with him, as she remembered her mother telling her how much she loved her father. So why didn't she remember him?

Deciding to go to bed, she had a restless night's sleep spent tossing and turning.

The next few days passed in a haze of work and she managed to catch up on so much she wore a self-satisfied look on her face. She called Claire and begged off Saturday night saying Boston was away on business and she had a company dinner she had forgotten about until she saw the email reminder.

Miserable because Boston was away and true to his word, Alyssa hadn't heard from him at all. She was at least grateful for the work dinner on Saturday to distract her from missing him.

Every so often Image West would take their employees out for dinner to show their appreciation for all their hard work. Partners weren't invited as these were purely for employees to just let loose.

The dinners were usually held at swanky restaurants or a place where the company's owner, Kurt Zellen felt everyone would enjoy. Like Alyssa, most of the employees at Image West enjoyed eating out at places they normally wouldn't.

Tonight, Kurt had organised dinner at Seafood and Steak, which had a casual atmosphere and was a very popular place. They had their own dining room so they could be as loud and as noisy as they liked.

The food was as delicious as everyone had come to expect since Kurt didn't ever pick restaurants with subpar food or service.

Alyssa was in the restroom freshening up when a group of women entered excitedly chatting.

"I can't believe how lucky you are, Ally."

"Yes, you've hit the jackpot with Neil. I hope he's got friends for me."

"Well, I think there's something not quite right about the guy."

"Oh Sans, you think that about every guy since —"

"Don't say his name," Sans scowled. "And I don't. Well, not always, but I'm telling you there's just something about Neil that's not quite genuine."

The names Ally and Neil felt familiar to Alyssa and yet no memory came to explain why she might recognise them. She had just left the restroom and hardly taken a step when she saw a man walking towards her coming from the direction of the men's restrooms.

Instantly her head spun as images she hadn't seen before burst forth into her mind...

Alyssa was coming out of the building elevator and saw Neil on his phone probably talking to his real girlfriend. Then she had the most surreal moment she'd ever had in her life. She locked eyes with someone she had never seen before and all of a sudden it was like she was in a dream world where they were the only two people in existence, yet she couldn't see his face, only his caramel eyes. Their conversation, which wasn't even spoken aloud but somehow telepathically, was completely bizarre especially since they were strangers and he had said, "I love you.".

Then Neil's voice broke the spell and he had given her roses. There was also something about his party and how he went behind her back and invited Uncle Jack so Alyssa had broken up with him.

Now the shock of seeing him was enough to trigger her memory of him and what he had done. *He* called her Ally, which just happened to also be the name of his other girlfriend, Alison. That's why she hated the name Ally, because of Neil.

"Hello Ally," he smiled, his eyes raking over her. "Good to see you again. It's been a while."

She stood there trying hard to pretend she wasn't shocked to see him.

"Neil. And it's Alyssa, not Ally," she said. "So are you and Alison here for dinner?" She didn't know why she asked the question, since she didn't even care who he was here with.

"Of course, why? Are you jealous?" He went to stroke her arm, but she took a step back.

"Doubt it," she snorted. "Well, I can't say it was good to see you again, Neil. Goodbye."

Turning on her heel, she went back into the restroom not caring if Neil was feeling smug at making her so uncomfortable that she now needed a minute to regroup.

"Hey, are you okay?" the women called Sans said. "You look pale and not well."

"I'm fine, just had a bit of dizziness hit," she said.

"There's a seat just outside. Come on, I'll help you there and then get you some water."

"No, no, I'm sure I'll be fine," she said, embarrassed by the fuss.

"Guys, I'm just going to help this lady so will see you back at the table, okay?" Sans said, to her friends.

"Okay," they said.

"I'm sorry to put you to so much trouble," Alyssa said, as the woman they called Sans helped her to the seat. Alyssa couldn't help but worryingly look around, relieved Neil had gone.

"It's no trouble. Can I tell whomever you're with that you're not feeling well?" Sans said.

"No, I'm at a work dinner, but I'm sure I'll be fine in a few minutes," she said.

"I'll be right back with some water. Don't move."

"Sure, and thank you once again."

"Not a problem."

The woman walked off to get Alyssa a glass of water and she felt relieved by the woman's kindness. She did need to sit and didn't want to make a fuss. She was also hoping that none of her work colleagues would see her because then she'd be under the microscope of their concern.

All she needed was a little quiet to make sense of her new memories and to get her thoughts in order.

The woman came back with a glass of water.

"Here you go. How are you feeling?"

"I'm better. Thank you. Your friends have gone back to your table," she said.

"Do you mind if I sit here for a minute? I'm actually not in any rush to head back."

"Of course not. I'm Alyssa by the way."

"Sandra."

"It's nice to meet you, Sandra. You've been very kind. I don't mean to be nosy, but is there a reason you don't want to be with your friends?" she said, before realising it sounded just like that.

"No, it's okay," Sandra sighed. "You see, if you didn't hear us earlier, but my friend Alicia has got a new boyfriend, Neil, but there's just something about him that puts me off. It's not that he's sleazy or a jerk but, I don't know." She shook her head showing her confusion. "And I know everyone thinks I'm being super cynical because my last boyfriend cheated on me, but I swear it's not that. There's just something about this guy I have a bad feeling about."

"Well, I dated a Neil once," Alyssa said, not wanting to mention that she had also just run into the lying cheater. "It turned out that he was cheating on his girlfriend with me, which I hadn't realised until later. Her name was Alison and mine is Alyssa so he called us both Ally."

"Oh my God," Sandra gasped, shocked. "How did you find out?"

"Well, I accidentally overheard him talking to her and when I confronted him, he then told me I was his one and only and had dumped her," she said. "As it turned out, he was only using me to get a promotion because my uncle is well-known. He even said that he wanted to marry me."

"Oh no, I'm so sorry. At least you found out in time."

"That's the one thing I'm thankful for," she said.

"If you don't mind my asking, what was your Neil's surname?"

"Jones."

Sandra's gasp of shock made Alyssa have that sinking feeling. Was Neil up to his old tricks? He said he was with Alison tonight or was that just a lie to get his own back on her?

"It's the same Neil, isn't it?" she sympathised.

"I think so," Sandra said.

"Tallish, brown hair and eyes?"

"Yes."

"Your friend doesn't have business connections to the place Neil works at?" she said.

"I don't think so. Her whole family are lawyers, except for her. Just to be sure, where does your ex work?" Sandra said.

"Oh, I don't know if he's still there, but it was Freight Forward,"she said.

"Hmm, Alicia's Neil works for Anderson Management."

"Well then, it may not be the same man," she said, relieved she hadn't ruined someone's relationship by accident. Still, she couldn't help feeling that her ex was the same Neil.

"By any chance is Neil here tonight?" she said.

"Yes."

"I don't suppose he's wearing a dark suit with blue shirt?"

"Well yes, but so are a lot of men," Sandra said.

That was true, just as Alyssa's description of Neil could be any man. Taking a deep breath, she confessed.

"My ex is here tonight. I just ran into him before, which is why I wasn't feeling too good."

"Do you still love him?" Sandra said.

"Oh God no," she said, emphatic. "It was more of a shock since it was the first time I've seen him since we broke up." It wasn't quite a fib, but she wasn't about to try and explain her memory loss to a stranger.

"I don't suppose you'd come and see if it is the same person," Sandra said.

"Oh, I don't want to ruin —"

"*Please*," Sandra said. "Just come and peek and if it isn't him, we can laugh about it. I don't want my friend ending up with some guy who's using her. I doubt she'd believe me if I told her what you said."

"But we don't know if he's using her. He may truly

love your friend," she said.

"Or he could be cheating on his other girlfriend like he did with you in hopes that Alicia won't found out."

"I don't know. I don't think this is a good idea. What happens if we ruin her relationship?"

"Okay, how about this. You look at our table from afar and tell me if you see your Neil. If it's the same guy, then I'll ask Alicia to come here and speak to you."

"No," she said, shaking her head. "I'm sorry, but I'll only see if it's the same Neil."

"Fine, I'll take it," Sandra said, resigned. "I hope we're wrong about this."

"So do I."

They went and found a discreet distance to look at the table Sandra was on and Alyssa's heart sank. Alicia's Neil and hers were one and the same.

"I'm sorry, but that guy is definitely the same guy I dated. Now, I really do need to get back to my friends. Thank you for all your help," Alyssa said.

"No, thank you. Now I'll be watching Neil like a hawk," Sandra said.

"Well, good luck," Alyssa said, heading back to her table.

As she sat there, Alyssa couldn't quite get her inter-action with Sandra out of her head. Should she have confronted Neil for Sandra's friend or had she done the right thing? The only reason this had all happened was because she got her memory of him back, otherwise she'd

have been none the wiser. She shouldn't butt into someone else's relationship however, she just couldn't seem to
shake the feeling that Neil was once again cheating with
this woman since Sandra had said her name was Alicia.

Knowing she was now sitting at dinner, but not as
jovial as before, Alyssa was relieved when the night was
ending.

Going home, Alyssa was miserable. While she was
happy to have finally slammed the door shut on Neil after
seeing him again. Knowing she had a lucky escape by
dumping the jerk, who may be up to his old tricks again,
her only regret was Boston hadn't been here to also throw
in Neil's face that she had moved onto a better man. Plus
she also missed Boston. His not calling had left a hole in
her life she didn't even realise he'd made. Perhaps she
had been too quick and judgmental about him.

Comparing Boston and Neil wasn't even a compe-
tition. Boston won hands down. He was a hundred times
the boyfriend Neil had been in a week alone. Mind you,
that wasn't hard since Neil was a lying cheater.

Still moping over last night's run in with Neil and
missing Boston, she was cleaning out her handbag when
she came across his business card.

Looking at it, some sort of quick weird flashback was
happening, but not like her other ones. This was just
voices and no faces and the fright made her drop the card
as if it burned her. Staring at it on the ground, unsure what
was happening, she knew it was Boston's card, yet she

was sure the memory from it wasn't him, which left her shaking at who the hell was she remembering.

Unsure what this all meant, she tossed between calling and not calling him until she made herself feel seasick with all her lurching, before telling herself to stop being a chicken and to just call. Surely he would want to hear from her, she convinced herself. She could either just leave a message or maybe just play it really cool and casual like she forgot he was away.

Yes, she could do that. Hesitantly, she dialled the number and hoped he wouldn't be mad at the interruption.

"Boston Chan," he said, yet to Alyssa it didn't sound like him, maybe the line was funny.

"Hi Boston. It's Alyssa," she said, nervous

"Alyssa? Oh, Alyssa, I was wondering when you were going to call."

"You were?" she said, confused.

"Of course. We should catch up. How's Friday night?"

"Aren't you away on business?"

"Yes, but I'll be back by Friday night," he said.

"Okay, I'll see you Friday night."

Alyssa pushed her bewilderment aside about the conversation she'd just had. Was she the one who got her wires crossed and Boston hadn't been ignoring her, he had just been busy.

The world seemed sunny again and she couldn't wait until Friday.

Chapter Twelve

Boston lied to Alyssa when he said he was away on business. Well, it was really more a fudging of the truth. He was away on business, but he was also using this trip to see his sister and new nephew. He would have asked Alyssa to come however, knew Indi would not only be asking a million uncomfortable and highly improbable unanswerable questions all the while reading more into him bringing Alyssa than necessary. Also Alyssa herself, would probably read more into the trip. Besides, she was back at work and he was pretty sure her employer wouldn't appreciate her taking even more time off for a spur-of-the-moment holiday.

These were all the justifications he used to ease any guilt he was feeling.

"Bos!" Indi squealed, ecstatic to see her brother and

hugging him tightly to her. "It's been too long and you haven't called in a while. Between you and me, I think Jason still misses chatting to you all the time, although now with children he'd probably use it as time out from the chaos."

"I miss talking to him too," he chuckled. It was nice having an older brother to chew the fat with. "And he can always come over and visit to get away."

Indi shot him one of her classic, over my dead body looks, making him laugh.

"Your timing couldn't be better. Mon's here visiting as well," she said.

Hearing Montana was also here he was doubly relieved he hadn't brought Alyssa as both sisters would definitely be ganging up on him no matter what. There was also all their meddling and together, they were expert interrogators and thus if Alyssa were here, it would be like leaving a poor defenceless newborn lamb to some vicious coyotes.

At least he knew their tactics and could employ his own to fend them off, which took a lot of focus and concentration when they were two against one and he had no back-up.

"Are you sure you're okay with so many visitors?" he said, worried Indi might be overdoing it.

"Are you kidding? Having a baby means Jason not only treats me like a queen, but I've got so many people helping out, all I do is look after the baby, that is if I can pry him away from Jason, who keeps hogging him," she laughed.

"How's Mon?" he said.

"Here for the weekend and you know Mon, she's being as bossy as ever," she said, rolling her eyes in disgust. "I've forgotten how bossy she can be."

"Oh well, that's what you get for only being the *second* eldest," he teased. "Now where is my new nephew and more importantly, is he cute?"

"Very," she giggled. "Makes me want a truckload more."

"Ew, too much information. I don't need to know," he chuckled, screwing up his face.

"Yes, you do," she teased. "Come on, everyone's going to be happy you're here."

She led him into the lounge and seeing everyone's face light up at his arrival made him feel so loved and at the same time miss them all.

"Bos! You're finally here. Come and meet your new nephew," Jason said, placing the baby into Boston's arms after everyone hugged him.

"He's so tiny and cute." He looked down in awe at the newest member of the Chan/Kwong Lee clan. "Are you sure it's Jason's because he looks more like Nix, not a Kwong Lee," he grinned.

"Very funny," Jason said, taking his son back.

"Did you bring your kids?" he said to Montana, look-ing around for her children.

"Jason's sister was here and they offered to take all the kids and who were we to say no to some kid-free time," Montana smiled. "Besides, we didn't realise that you were coming over, otherwise we would have kept them with us."

"Sorry, it was a surprise visit. Not that you mentioned coming over either," he teased.

"We were a last minute decision also. But since you're here and there's no kids, tell us what's going on in your life?" Montana said, and the interrogation began.

He wasn't sure if he wanted to let his sisters know all about Alyssa just yet and so he kept his recounting as bland and boring as possible.

"Not a lot to tell. I've just been busy working as usual," he said.

"No new girlfriend?" Indi said. "What happened to the girl you met just a few weeks ago?"

"What girl?" he said, trying to hide his shock Indi knew about Alyssa.

"I can't remember, you told Jase about her," Indi said.

Now he frowned. He hadn't told anyone about Alyssa so who was Indi referring to? Oh, that's right, he remembered. Sasha, the woman who would have been his latest quick fling if he hadn't met Alyssa.

"Oh her, yeah, that was nothing," he said.

His sisters didn't look impressed with his honesty as Jason and Lucas just smiled to themselves.

"Bos, you need to find a woman and *settle* down," Indi scolded.

"Yes, you can't just keep having flings. You'll never know if she's the right woman for you otherwise," Montana said.

"Says the woman who had a *fling* and is now married with children to him," he laughed.

"It wasn't like that," Montana huffed.

"He's got you there, tesoro," Lucas grinned, giving his wife a kiss.

Since the baby needed feeding, Indi and Montana left the room, giving Boston and his brothers-in-law a chance to catch up in private.

"So how's it really going, Bos?" Lucas said.

He looked furtively around to make sure his sisters were definitely out of earshot before answering.

"If I tell you, do you two promise not to tell Mon or Indi?"

"You know the rule, if it's anything dangerous or life-threatening, or more importantly if your sister asks, you know I can't keep secrets from her," Lucas said.

"Ditto. You don't want to be in the doghouse with a Chan sister," Jason nodded.

Boston sighed, shaking his head at their stupid family rules that they made up or altered when it suited. They all used them and were okay with them as long as they were the ones *hearing* the secret, not the ones to *speak* it.

"And you know Mon's going to ask if you said

anything to us, she always does. I'll fudge around it however, if she pulls out the big guns and uses her eldest sister/mother-hen tone, I'll cave in an instant," Lucas chuckled.

"Same with Indi. Although she is more distracted because of the baby," Jason grinned.

"I know," he sighed. "But I do need a sounding board. And yes, I know my sisters will find out, but first I need to get my own head around what it all means."

"Fair enough. I'm sure Jase and I can hold them off as long as possible, but you know your sisters, I'll give you till dinner before you cave and are blurting out your woes," Lucas smiled.

"Thanks for the vote of confidence," he said.

"You're their brother and a *younger* one at that. That gives them all kinds of power to abuse and you know them, they just give you a look and you'll be confessing. I've even seen it happen over the phone," Jason laughed.

"And as we are also younger brothers to elder sisters, we've seen and understand our wives are on a completely different level to our own sisters, so we'll be cracking the first moment they give us one of *those* looks," Lucas said.

"Of course, you'd manage to hold out longer, but not us two," Jason said.

That was so true. Even on opposite sides of the world, his older sisters could break their siblings. He had heard his younger siblings' complaints often enough to know it was true.

"Fine," he sighed. "Where do I start?"

"At the beginning," Lucas said, getting comfortable.

Silently Jason and Lucas both hoped this was personal and not business. As weird as many people thought, they actually didn't have any worries about Boston's business capabilities. He was cautious enough when required and was always thorough in his dealings and research.

Some people thought the men were crazy to have invested in not only a family member who was green and untried, but one who made decisions on a gut feeling. However, they didn't know Boston like Lucas and Jason did.

Not once had Lucas or Jason regretted giving Boston the money to start his business or truly looked over his shoulder to make sure everything was going okay. In fact, they were more than impressed at his intuitive sense of business. Boston, for his part, appreciated their faith and trust in him and therefore found it easy to ask any tricky business questions or advice knowing Lucas or Jason would be honest in their answers.

Even when Boston made the odd bad investment or missed out on a golden opportunity, Jason and Lucas never made Boston feel bad about it because they too, had made many a mistake themselves. At those times, all they did was remind him that it was a teaching moment and to learn from it, which also helped Boston to become an even more successful businessman.

Now Boston was becoming a force to reckon with in

the business world and yet, still single with no long-term partner in sight. Both Jason and Lucas knew Montana and Indiana only wanted their brother to have the same happy work/life balance Jason and Lucas had with their wives.

"So a really weird thing happened recently where the hospital rang to tell me my girlfriend had an accident and had been admitted," Boston said.

Lucas frowned. He thought Boston just said he didn't have a girlfriend. Knowing he needed to hear the entire story, he didn't interrupt with all his curious questions.

"So I stayed the week with her and now I'm here," Boston said, recapping his situation with Alyssa.

And soon as Boston finished his story, Lucas and Jason instantly knew the exact reactions their wives were about to have. They were going to be ecstatic Boston had finally found *his one*. To be honest, both men thought it too. It seemed nobody in the Chan family knew what a normal courtship was and Boston was no exception.

"So let me get this straight, you have some kind of otherworldly, out of body experience upon first seeing Alyssa and then out of the blue, the hospital calls *you* to let you know your 'girlfriend's' had some kind of accident," Lucas said, amazed by Boston's story.

"A girlfriend you didn't have or even know about," Jason said.

"Who just happens to be the same woman of your mystical meeting, and then you kindly did the right thing by staying with her until she got back on her feet, even though you didn't have to —" Lucas said.

"By pretending you were her boyfriend, even though she has partial amnesia and doesn't have a clue who you are. So, the big question we don't know the answer to, is how she's going to react if she does get her memory back and realises that she had never met you before the accident. I hate to say it, but I'm thinking some screaming, possibly angry yelling at you are good odds," Jason said.

"I was trying to be nice," he said, defensive, but deep down knew Jason was right.

"Do you think she's faking it?" Lucas said.

"What? Why?" he said.

"Ah, take a look in the mirror," Jason said, the light bulb switching on as soon as Lucas mentioned it. "You are Boston Chan, handsome and successful. It wouldn't be the first time a woman played this kind of trick to try and snag a wealthy, eligible bachelor."

Lucas nodded. Both he and Jason and their families had seen this kind of manipulation over the years, and had even been subjected to a few of these tricks themselves.

"Lys wouldn't do that. She's not faking," he said, belligerent.

"Then what's the problem?" Lucas said.

"I don't know," he said, raking a hand through his hair. "It's just all gone all weird."

"Weird? How?" Lucas frowned.

"Ever since I moved out and she went back to work,

it's like we've lost that connection."

"I don't know what to say," Lucas said, as Boston looked miserable. "What I do know is that your sisters are about to be jumping up and down in joyful glee, beyond ecstatic that you've finally found *the one*."

Jason was impressed Lucas was willing to state the fact out loud. Even more telling was the fact Boston didn't even try to deny it, which spoke volumes to the men in the room. Clearly their brother-in-law also thought Alyssa was *his one* or at least wanted her to be.

"And true to Chan family form, the whole thing is complicated. Yet another great Chan family love story to add to the book," Jason grinned.

"I agree," Lucas smiled. "Can't wait to see how this story goes. However, I think we should warn you that it's probably going to get a lot muckier before you see the light at the end of the tunnel."

"So true," Jason said.

"What do you mean?" Boston said, puzzled.

"Well, you know our stories. True love is *never* simple," Lucas said.

"And if it was, then it wouldn't be as much fun," Jason smiled.

"Although when you're living through it, it's absolutely horrible. A nightmare," Lucas grinned.

"Can even be traumatising," Jason chuckled.

"But we've only just met," Boston said, confused.

"Exactly, which means you still have a lot of the rollercoaster ride left to go," Lucas said.

"Not to mention the biggest elephant in the room. What happens when Alyssa gets her memory back and realises the truth, that you've been lying to her," Jason said.

"But she might not remember," Boston said, grabbing at thin air and hoping that moment never came. It was too frightening to think about.

"And that's why it *will* happen. Chan family relationships 101. There's bound to be an explosion somewhere in it. This will be yours. Mark my words," Lucas said.

"But don't worry," Jason said, trying to cheer Boston up. "You know we'll always have your back."

"Plus, you have meddling sisters," Lucas laughed.

"What does that mean?" Boston said, hesitant and a little afraid.

"That means when it all blows up, they'll be jumping in with both feet to aid true love's happily ever after."

Boston groaned at the thought his older sisters would somehow be inserting themselves into his love-life. Could anything be more embarrassing than that? Then he remembered that Montana had Lucas and even Lucas' cousin insert themselves into the Indi and Jason reconciliation drama and therefore what his brothers-in-law just said was true. If this all turned pear-shaped then his family would be putting their meddling noses in, no matter what. He also wouldn't be getting a say in the matter and once again, that was the annoying thing about having a close family.

True to his brothers-in-law's earlier words, Boston managed to last until after dinner, but only because he managed to divert the conversation to catch up on every family member whether it be Chan, Romero or Kwong Lee to buy himself some time. Silently Lucas and Jason both thought it was a pretty clever trick and helped him to drag out the conversation so the sisters couldn't really get a foothold in their interrogation.

The men were impressed by the sisters' subtle manoeuvrings as if they were bloodhounds with a scent. Knowing Montana and Indi weren't about to easily give up, as soon as dinner finished the interrogation ramped up so they couldn't be put off any longer.

"All right, let's have it," Indi huffed.

"Have what?" Boston said, feigning innocence.

"Oh please, we know something's going on. Make it quick before the baby needs another feed otherwise I'll be doing it here, right in front of you," she said, making Boston look appalled. "I'll be covered." She rolled her eyes as he looked relieved.

Both Jason and Lucas just sat there looking a picture of perfect innocence.

"There's nothing going on," Boston huffed.

"Sure there's not," Indi said, sensing his lie. "Just like you needed to come and visit us, right now."

"It was just good timing I had some business over this way and wanted to catch up with you guys and meet my newest nephew, that's all," he said, trying to deflect his sisters, but was beginning to squirm.

"Bos!" Montana growled. "Don't make me sit on you and box your ears in."

"As if," he snorted.

"I'll do it," Indi said. "He wouldn't dare retaliate against a new mother and besides, Jason wouldn't let him either, would you honey?"

The pointed look his wife gave him made Jason squirm.

"Of course not. Oh, is that the baby I hear?" Jason said.

"Chicken," Boston said, under his breath as everyone laughed.

"Maybe, but when you have a wife, then we'll see just how brave you are," Jason said.

"Lucas?" Montana now gave her husband a pointed look.

"Hey, don't look at me. I'm Switzerland." He held his hands up in surrender.

"Then you sit on him so I can box his ears," Montana smiled.

"You're on your own Bos, I tried," Lucas laughed.

"Fine," he sighed. To be honest, he wouldn't mind his sisters unwanted advice, yet he wasn't about to let them know that, so he acted resigned to his fate. "I met this woman who —"

"I knew it," Montana crowed. "Told you Indi, didn't I. He's finally found *the one*."

"And I told you I agreed," Indi smiled. The two sisters looked very pleased with themselves.

"Carry on Bos, tell us about your future *wife*," Jason teased, as if he didn't know any of the story.

"Yes, tell us *everything*," Montana said, sitting forward eager hear what Boston had to say.

"Her name's Alyssa and I met her…"

As predicted once he finished his story, his sisters were both wistfully sighing.

"That's so romantic," Montana said, hugging Lucas who kissed the top of her head.

"So romantic," Indi sighed, as Jason copied Lucas' actions with his wife.

Watching his sisters so happy and in love left Boston suddenly feeling very alone.

"So what am I going to do?" he sighed.

"There's really only one thing to do," Montana said. "You have to tell her the truth."

"Put all your cards on the table and confess," Indi said.

"But what if she wants nothing to do with me ever again?" he said, anxious.

"I highly doubt that. Sure, she'll be angry and hurt, but then she'll see just how right you two are together," Montana said, showing her wisdom.

"You may have to do a bit of grovelling as well," Indi said, wanting to make sure Boston didn't think that it would blow over just like that.

"What would you guys do, if you were me?" he said,

looking at his brothers-in-law.

"Probably the same thing you're doing. Be in a bit of denial and too chicken to tell her," Lucas said, knowing from experience that confessing your sins wasn't as simple as in the movies.

"He's right, Bos," Jason said. "You're going to have to get your courage up because confessing and knowing her reaction won't be one of happiness and joy, is a pretty scary prospect."

"But she'll get over it," Montana said, supportive.

"I agree with Jase, you'll have to find your courage because as you know, it's hard to confess," Lucas said, reminding his wife that their courtship wasn't exactly plain sailing and Montana had her ex-brother-in-law do the dirty work and confess her secret for her to Lucas, along with Indi's meddling.

"It's true, Bos. Believe me, I've been where you are and you will drive yourself mad thinking of every scenario and then deciding when the right time to tell her is. And, believe me, there is *no* right time. That's just something that happens in the movies. I get it though. It does take a lot to try and summon all your courage to make a confession of this magnitude. However, you're just going to have to bite the bullet and tell her, that is if she truly means that much to you," Montana said.

"Do you love her?" Indi said. "You sound like you do to us, but what does your heart say?"

These were all the questions he needed to hear. Did he

love Alyssa? He thought he did. Still he didn't really have an answer.

"I don't really know. I mean, I think so. It's just that I've never truly been in love before, so I have no idea," he sighed, raking a hand through his hair. "I do know that being with her makes me feel calm and peaceful. I'm not always thinking of work and am happy to just be."

"Do you always think about her or want to be with her, even if it's sitting in silence," Indi said.

"Yes."

"Then that's love," Montana said, as everyone in the room nodded.

After talking to his family, Boston did some reflecting on his trip mostly about Alyssa. She deserved to know the truth, that they had never met and the only reason he was at the hospital was they called him by mistake. They definitely weren't dating, but he wanted to. His family were right, she did constantly invade his thoughts and he had picked up the phone so many times to call her before chickening out. Then he justified not calling and telling her by thinking it was something which needed to be said face to face. He also didn't realise just how much he would miss her. Sure, it was only a few weeks, but after being with her effectively twenty/four seven for a week, Alyssa had become a part of him.

Not being one to need pep talks, he was a man of action. Someone who got things done. He was Boston Chan, a very successful businessman who always got what he wanted, so why he was being so insecure about Alyssa, he had no idea. The more he thought about it, the more he realised he was being a coward instead of the normal take charge guy he was known for.

Yes, when he got back, he was going to lay his cards on the table and then begin a proper relationship with his angel.

Chapter Thirteen

This morning Alyssa was buzzing with nervous energy. Wanting to dress so she would be able to go straight from work to dinner, she decided upon black trousers and a maroon-coloured blouse. Now she was touching up her make-up before grabbing her handbag and leaving work.

Her excitement at seeing Boston again was palpable. She couldn't stop smiling. Arriving at the restaurant, she looked around for him.

"Alyssa, you look beautiful. I'm so glad you could make it," he said, behind her and she spun around full of excitement.

Her bright smile instantly vanished as she stared in horror at the man smiling at her as her mind burst into a million images all at once featuring this man.

Here's my card. I have to go. Can I get you a drink? I'm Boston Chan.

On and on the flashes of memory came zooming back to her as the blood drained from her face and she swayed, and a terrifying thought hit her. If the man in front of her was Boston Chan, then who the hell was the guy she had spent a week with, made love to and even fallen in love with?

"Alyssa, are you okay?" Boston quickly went to catch her. This Boston Chan's look of worry and concern helped to ease the shock.

No wonder she couldn't remember the other Boston. She had never met him before. That Boston even joked about trawling the hospital to find someone who had lost their memory. At the time it had been a funny joke, now all it left was a horrified nightmare. And hadn't he said they only just met? They sure had. Literally.

As she looked into the eyes of this Boston, Alyssa didn't feel the same energy or connection she had with the other Boston however, at least, she felt comfortable and safe.

"I-I'm fine. I think I've just got low blood sugar. I-I'll be fine once I've eaten."

The maître d' quickly showed them to a table and she was relieved to sit down.

Now as they ate dinner, Alyssa couldn't help but look across the table at Boston. He made her laugh telling her funny story after funny story and when it came time to leave, she felt like she knew so much about him, she didn't want the evening to end.

The only similarity between the two Bostons besides their name was they were both good-looking. However, one blatantly lied to her face and the other hadn't. One, she now remembered, whereas the other never existed.

"Would you like to come back to my hotel for a drink?" he said, as he helped her put her jacket on.

"Your hotel?" she said, surprised by the location.

"Yes, I own it. It's full at the moment so I've only got a normal room instead of a suite since my house is being renovated."

"Oh, wouldn't they give you a suite if you own it?" she said, slightly puzzled.

"Of course, but there's people willing to pay good money for a suite so why deprive them of that. I don't mind a normal room as I don't need much space."

Granted it was practical, but the fact he wasn't throwing his weight around like he could if he really wanted to, made Alyssa melt at how humble he seemed.

"I'd love to," she said, her voice husky as he smiled.

Before Alyssa even comprehended what was happening, one moment he was asking if she still wanted that drink and the next, they were tearing each other's clothes off in the elevator.

They ran laughing all the way to his room before someone saw them in a dishevelled state of semi-undress. Once inside his room, it didn't take long for their clothes to come off and Boston was making love to her.

Afterwards Alyssa lay there thinking of the two Bostons. Since she couldn't keep calling them by the same name as it was confusing even to her, she decided to call the Boston she remembered, RB for remembered or real Boston and FB for fake Boston.

Not knowing what FB's real agenda was, she decided she was going to turn the tables on him and string him along until she either found out his true intentions or she taught him a lesson for thinking she was an easy target.

She was going to make FB wish he'd never picked her or anyone else to play this trick on again.

Feeling a lot better now she had a plan, she teased the real Boston awake with her mouth and began round two.

On Tuesday RB phoned to say he had another business trip planned and wouldn't be back for a couple of weeks. Although Alyssa was disappointed, his absence meant she could now put her plan into action without him ever knowing he was being impersonated. She could have just told him there was an impostor posing as him, but she took this as her way of defending her man. It was just FB's bad luck she happened to not only remember the real Boston, but had also met up with him.

Ignoring the niggling feeling that this wasn't the wisest course of action and she should just confront FB and tell him that she knew he was a fraud, for some reason she just didn't want to. She didn't want to think that it was so she could keep sleeping with FB because she knew that should now revolt her. Nevertheless, she guiltily felt a sense of excitement about not only seeing him again, but also the possibility of sex. Alyssa just hoped she was able to play the game and keep her heart intact.

Let the games begin.

After two weeks away and missing Alyssa, as soon as Boston landed and knowing it was a Friday night, he decided to take the chance Alyssa would be home. Grabbing a bouquet of flowers, he headed straight over to her place and rapped on the door, hoping to surprise her.

Alyssa, who was in her tracksuit peeked out through the eyehole to see the fake Boston standing there. She ignored the fact her heart skipped a beat and quickly ran to her room and yelled she was coming while changing as fast as possible into the sexiest dress she could grab.

"You're early," she said, opening the door wide then trying to look shocked to see him.

Boston just stood there drinking in the sight of his sexy angel who he had missed terribly, if he was admitting the truth to himself.

"Hi," he smiled.

"Boston! You're back. Why didn't you tell me?" she squealed, excitedly jumping on him to hug him tightly. She then kissed him as passionately as possible trying hard to remember he was a lying scoundrel, but as he deepened it, she felt her body have the same traitorous reaction it always did with him. She pulled away before she did something stupid like sleep with him.

"I wanted to surprise you. Ah, were you expecting someone else?" he said, knowing the sexy dress she was wearing wasn't for him although he appreciated the way it hugged all her curves.

"You have," she said, ignoring his question and taking the flowers from him as he entered the room.

"How have you been?" What he really wanted to ask was if she missed him.

"Great. How was your trip?"

"Great." He looked around to see if there was another man here or was she planning on going out on a date.

"Are you going somewhere?"

"Girls' night out. I didn't realise you'd be home tonight, but I don't have to go. I can cancel on them," she said, making him want to say yes.

Since he was the one who surprised her, he couldn't ruin her plans even if he wished Alyssa would change her dress. She'd have men all over her and he firmly ignored the jealous possessiveness he felt.

"No, no. You go and have fun. It's my own fault for wanting to surprise you. So how's your memory coming along?" he said.

"So-so. Actually since you brought it up, some of my friends were asking things about you and I didn't know what to say," she said.

"Oh?"

"How did we meet again? Where was our first date? Who asked who out?" she said, waiting for his answer and watching him closely.

Boston felt like he was on hot coals at her questions.

"Well, we met in your building foyer and I believe I asked you out. You tried to resist me, play hard to get, but my charm wore you down until you gave in." His grin made her melt until she reminded herself, he was a liar. "Our first date was a picnic and by the time we finished, I knew I had fallen in love with you."

Alyssa wanted to give him an Oscar for that fine performance. If she hadn't met the real Boston, she would have believed every word hook, line and sinker.

"That's so romantic," she sighed, hoping it sounded genuine. "So did you say 'I love you' first?"

"Actually neither of us have said it."

"Oh, but —"

"Just because I knew it, doesn't mean I came right out and said it. It was our first date. I didn't know if you felt the same strong connection and I didn't want to scare you off," he said.

"Well, I guess I must feel it too, otherwise why would we even be dating, right?" Seeing him look uncomfortable made her happy.

"I'd better go and let you finish getting ready. Enjoy your night out," he said, giving her a peck on the cheek before leaving.

She wanted to yell, 'liar' and 'impostor' after him and

even felt a strong urge to throw something at him, but didn't dare. She didn't want to ruin her plan and firmly squashed down the fact that upon seeing him again, her whole body reacted with happiness.

So much for telling her the truth, you chicken, Boston chided himself as he walked away from Alyssa's feeling weighed down. She was beginning to ask more questions, which he hated having to lie about and realised this was what everyone had been trying to warn him about.

He also wasn't too crazy about her casual attitude about whether she felt the same for him. It actually hurt. Maybe this was karma's way of teaching him a lesson as never once had he truly loved any of the women he'd dated and yet, those women easily bandied 'I love you' to him all the time. Now the woman with amnesia who meant the most to him, was the one who seemed to give tiny cuts, which hurt as much as if he'd been stabbed. Maybe Alyssa Lee wasn't a nice person at all. Maybe she was a selfish, self-centred person, yet he knew he didn't believe that at all.

Alyssa waited half an hour before changing into her pyjamas to make sure Boston didn't come back. She refused to feel any guilt or regret she was now the one lying and playing games when he had started this whole charade to begin with.

Next, she was going to make him retrace some of the

supposed things they'd done together to see what creative answers he could come up with. Yes, she was looking forward to teaching him a lesson. She also needed to make sure they did a couples' night with Liz and Claire because her friends had met the real Boston. She'd let them in on her little scheme knowing they'd help and even possibly stir the situation up a little. A smile crossed her lips.

Her alarm was beeping and she groaned rolling over to hit the snooze button so she could go back to sleep before remembering why her alarm was going off at three thirty in the morning.

Groggily she found her cell phone to call Boston.

Hearing the phone ring and ring a sleepy voice finally picked up.

"Hello?" the sleepy voice said.

"Hi honey," she giggled. "Are you sleeping, you old fuddy duddy?"

"Lys? It's three thirty in the morning," Boston groaned.

"Don't be such a party pooper."

"Did you have a good time with the girls?"

"Of course. You should have seen the hot guys hitting on us. They were *so* cute. I could have just eaten them up with a spoon and they bought me so many drinks," she giggled.

"Lys, are you drunk?"

Boston was now wide awake with her rambling about hot guys and a quiet anger was simmering inside him. She better not have gone home with anyone.

"Silly, of course I'm not. But shush, don't tell anyone I can't remember anything," she giggled.

"Lys, did you bring anyone home with you?" He hadn't wanted to ask, but since she was drunk he hoped she might not even remember this conversation.

"Um, Oli kissed me, he's *such* a good kisser. Or was it, Dan? I can't remember although I'm sure I have his number somewhere. Don't worry I got home all by myself, I'm a big girl."

"You let some guys kiss you?" Boston's rage was starting to boil.

"Who are you, my father? Oh wait, you could be because I don't remember him. Are you?"

"No, I'm not."

"I wish Steve had come home with me because he was the hottest and I'm *so* horny," she said, in her sexiest whisper and then the line went silent.

"Lys! Lys!"

Boston sat bolt upright, worried something happened to Alyssa. Then he could faintly hear her singing and the tap going before he heard what sounded like a flop onto the bed.

The silence worried him, was she asleep or had she forgotten she was on the line? He called her name over and over, but nothing.

Frustrated by her lack of an answer, he didn't know if he should go over to her place, but if she was asleep there was no way he could get in, and he presumed pounding on the door wasn't going help because she wouldn't hear him. It would also probably wake up the neighbours.

Resigned, he disconnected the call and now couldn't sleep. She had gone out and got drunk, kissed random men and even told him she wanted sex.

God, he was tormented. He should never have let her out in that dress. If he had seen her in that dress in a club, he would have been all over her like a rash, only she would have gone home with him and he would have had sex with her.

He felt out of control and aroused. Getting up, he went and had a long cold shower.

Alyssa heard Boston disconnect the phone and giggled. Letting him believe she went out and got drunk, kissed lots of guys and was hot for sex was mean, but he deserved it. She half expected him to come storming over and pound on her door demanding to be let in and there was a sense of disappointment he hadn't. Not that she would have let him in. She would have pretended she was asleep, dead to the world.

Still giggling to herself, she fell back to sleep ignoring the little seed of guilt.

At eight in the morning there was loud pounding on her door and it woke Alyssa up. Smiling to herself because she automatically knew who it had to be and made sure she looked really sleepy and dishevelled before going to the door.

"What?" she groaned, squinting through the crack in

the door as if she couldn't stand the light.

A shadow fell over her as Boston entered her apartment with a scowl on his face as Alyssa hid a gleeful smile.

"Boston! What are you doing here so early?" she moaned, going into her kitchen to grope for a glass to get some water.

Seeing Alyssa dishevelled and looking hungover, he decided to take pity on her and followed her into the kitchen.

He'd been so tormented for the rest of the night that he had tossed and turned and by five in the morning got up to do some work, knowing sleep was the last thing on his mind. Even this didn't work to distract his thoughts, so as soon as decently possible, he headed to Alyssa's.

"I thought you might like breakfast," he said, not mentioning her call at three thirty in the morning.

"It's eight o'clock," she groaned again, smothering her smile by taking a drink of water.

"So how was your night?"

That elicited another groan from her and she slowly made her way to the couch and lay down on it.

"I can't remember, my head hurts."

"You don't remember anything?"

"No, we went to a club and it was packed and hot, that's all I remember."

"So meet any guys?" He hated himself for asking what he already knew, but he wanted to see her face this time.

Alyssa couldn't believe how good her acting skills were and wondered if perhaps she had missed her calling by being in marketing instead of an actress.

"I don't remember. I think there were a few guys hitting on us, but since we're all taken, I think we just strung them along for the free drinks. Look, I would love to tell you all about it, but I'm tired and need to go back to bed."

"Good idea," he said, scooping her up to her squeals and taking her to bed.

He not only took her breath away with the determination of his lovemaking, but also made her feel guilty about two-timing the real Boston. Nevertheless, she couldn't deny this Boston definitely knew how to make love to her.

"What are you thinking?" he said, as her head lay on his chest. He was a lot happier now he made her writhe and scream in pleasure. She didn't even seem to mind he was a little bit wilder because of his jealousy.

"Why didn't you call while you were away?" She wanted to add, *you lying jerk*, yet didn't.

Alyssa sounded put out and it pleased him because it meant she missed him.

"I was really busy, but you could have called me if you needed to," he said, ignoring his guilt.

Oh, she had called him all right and it was just his terrible luck that she also found out the truth.

Before she could answer his lips found hers and he began distracting her from her thoughts.

Chapter Fourteen

To Alyssa's delight, her wish to have a couples' night with Boston came sooner than she thought and she didn't even have to plan it since he was the one to bring it up. Now she could snoop and hopefully get some answers and his friends would be none the wiser to her motives.

"My friends, Sam and Irene want to get together. They have some sort of couples' night where they invite three couples and play games. He asked if we wanted to join them?" Boston said, not really worried if she turned him down because it really wasn't his idea of fun.

"Sounds great. I'd love to meet your friends. Find out what you're really like," she teased.

"On second thoughts, maybe it's not such a good idea," he chuckled.

"When and where? I'll go by myself if I have to," she laughed.

"I'll pick you up. Friday at seven."

"I'll be ready."

When Sam called to catch up and told him about couples' night and he was a couple short, Boston volunteered him and Alyssa straight away, to both their surprise. He had never done a couples' night and hoped it went well.

Alyssa wondered what girlfriend type she should play before deciding to just be herself while ensuring she asked a lot of nosey questions. She wouldn't put it past Boston to have set this up to somehow reinforce he was Boston Chan. Unfortunately for him, he wouldn't be aware that she was going to use tonight as a way to hopefully find out more about his plan, which in turn could inadvertently help to trip him up.

She dressed simply in jeans and a blouse, and bought a bottle of wine to take. Opening the door to him, he looked sexy in jeans and the kiss was a million times hotter than she expected.

Remember he's up to something, using you, she firmly reminded herself before she got swept away once again.

"Mm, now that's a kiss. Maybe we should have our own couples' night private party," he said, his eyes darkening with desire.

"Sure."

Instead of going to her room, he took her hand and led her to the car.

"No, we'd better go. I don't want to let Sam and Irene

down," he said, knowing they could finish this later on.

Not after you've gone to all the trouble to set this up, Alyssa thought.

Sam and Irene had a lovely home and they were introduced to the two other couples there, Ed and Laura and Carl and Nicola.

"This is a lovely place you have, Irene," Alyssa said.

"Thank you, we've just done renovations."

Sam pulled Boston to one side.

"Are you kidding me? *You're* dating the hot woman who was being two-timed?"

"What can I say?" He shrugged with a cool confidence, which made Sam shake his head.

"So how did you two met?" Irene said, as Laura and Nicola listened as well.

"In the building foyer." She repeated what Boston told her, but her delivery was a statement of fact rather than romantic wistfulness and the other women picked up on it as she had hoped.

"Don't tell me the great Boston Chan has lost his touch? No big romantic sweep-you-off-your-feet gestures?" Irene said, surprised as the other women nodded.

"I guess not," Alyssa shrugged. "So how do you all know him?" she said, changing the subject.

"Oh, I've never met him before tonight, but I've heard tons about him, especially how hot and sexy he is," Nicola said, eyeing him over like he was dinner.

"Nic, that's rude especially in front of his girlfriend,"

Irene scolded, as Nicola just shrugged not really caring.

"But it's true. *He's hot.*"

"You'll have to excuse, Nic. She likes to ogle any and every man." Irene tried to apologise on Nicola's behalf, but Alyssa didn't care.

"I've known Boston for a few years. We don't see much of each other anymore," Laura said.

Alyssa knew exactly what that meant.

"So how long did you two date?"

"Only a few months," Laura said, a wistful look on her face.

Alyssa turned to Irene.

"Oh, I met him through Sam. They're good friends. He's a good man."

Irene was trying to smooth over the bumps in the conversation, relieved Alyssa didn't seem perturbed by the fact one woman was ogling her man and the other had dated him.

All Alyssa could think was that their role-playing was superb, just the right mix of personalities. She went and chatted to the men and Sam in particular seemed taken with her, yet she had no idea why.

"You look familiar, have we met before?" she said.

"No, but I've seen you around in the building foyer," Sam said.

"Oh, so you work in the Hightower Bank building too?"

"Level thirty-four."

Now it was all beginning to make sense. The reason Boston said they met in the lobby was because of Sam.

It was time to start playing games and it was Nicola who wanted to mix the teams up and claimed Boston much to Alyssa's amusement. Seeing Boston's annoyance she happily went along with the charade they were all playing for her sake, commenting she was honoured to partner Ed, who looked chuffed, while Laura's lips were tightly pursed.

She stifled a giggle wondering if she was supposed to have been partnering Sam so he could work whatever little magic he was supposed to on her, but Nicola ruined the pairings.

Boston, irritated by Nicola's hopeless attempts to try and hit on him, didn't complain since everyone else seemed happy with their partners so he kept fending her off until the next break.

"Okay, I want my girlfriend back," he said, as everyone stopped what they were doing to look at him.

"But we're a great team," Nicola said, smiling at him with desire in her eyes and he held back his irritation with her.

"Yeah, and Ally and I are winning," Ed said.

"She doesn't like being called Ally," he said, as Alyssa looked at him as if he had gone mad.

"Don't be silly. Ally is fine," she said to Ed, who looked taken aback by Boston's attitude. "We're almost finished. This is the last game so it's silly to switch teams now."

"She's right, Boston," Nicola said quickly, tightly holding herself to him until he managed to pry her off. Again, Carl seemed to take no notice of his girlfriend's flirtatiousness.

After what seemed like an eternity, the game finally finished with Alyssa and Ed the winners. Boston wanted to drag her out of Sam's however, Irene was serving coffees and dessert so he was forced to stay longer.

Alyssa used this time to try and gather more information on Boston since Nicola seemed to be occupying his time and was in no hurry to join the ladies for a chat. She just needed a way to get the ball rolling and it was Irene who inadvertently set it off.

"Wow, I've never seen Boston so uptight before. I swear he's jealous," Irene said, in a low voice.

"If I had known he liked attitude then I would have done it myself, but I thought he just liked beautiful women who are great at sex," Laura said, with a snide sting, annoyed Alyssa partnered her husband and won.

Irene gasped quietly at Laura's words and Alyssa couldn't help but make her own snide comment.

"Well, I guess he got a triple threat with me, then," she said, as Laura's face grew red with anger.

"So how long have you two been dating?" Irene said, quick to defuse the situation before it got out of hand.

"Not long. Tell me about him," Alyssa said.

"He dates a lot and then quickly loses interest." Laura gave Alyssa a pointed look which said, you won't be any different.

"Boston's a renown workaholic. Nothing comes between him and his company," Irene said.

"Except that one time," Laura said, giving Irene a sly smile.

"What time?" Irene said, feigning innocence.

"Oh, come on, Reen. You know."

Alyssa knew this was Laura's bitchy way to make her feel left out and uncomfortable.

"Oh, Mitzy," Irene said, her face red and Alyssa knew she didn't want to mention it, but thanks to Laura's bitterness the cat was now out of the bag.

"Whose Mitzy?" Alyssa said, intrigued to know whether Laura had thrown her grenade to not only blow up Boston's plans, but to also try and upset Alyssa.

"Oh, nobody, just an ex-girlfriend." Irene tried to politely end the enquiry.

Laura couldn't help but be a bitchy gossip since Boston's new girlfriend had shown her claws with her remark just before.

"Mitzy was Boston's *fiancée*," she said, gleeful as Alyssa's face whitened at her explanation. "We were all shocked he got engaged. I mean, he's hot in the sack, but that's where it normally ends, until Mitzy. Hey, you'll know since Sam and Bos are good buddies, but how did the engagement end?" Laura asked Irene like it was an innocent enough question, but also to twist the knife a bit more.

"Oh, I don't know," Irene tried to hedge but wasn't convincing enough for anyone.

"Come on Reen, tell us." Laura pushed her friend for an answer.

Irene glanced around to make sure no one else could hear them. She didn't like to gossip, but knew Laura wouldn't let it go because she was annoyed at Alyssa for not only partnering her husband, but also winning.

"He called it off saying he'd made a mistake. Mitzy then tried to get him back by making him jealous, but I've never known Boston to get jealous." She shot Alyssa a knowing look as a reminder about her earlier comment.

Alyssa didn't know if the women were playing good friend, bad ex-girlfriend for her benefit sharing private titbits about Boston, or maybe it was supposed to garner more sympathy towards him. What she did know was Laura was still bitter about being dumped by Boston and wanted to make sure Alyssa was also put in her place.

Finally Boston with his frustration at boiling point managed to get Alyssa out of the house. Everyone happily left Sam's at the same time saying, "We should all do this again sometime."

Boston's eyes rolled. There was no way in hell he was doing another couples' night, ever. Nicola tried to give him her cell phone number on the sly, but it was not only never going to happen as he just wasn't into her at all.

Alyssa or no Alyssa.

"Did you enjoy yourself tonight? You seemed happy chatting to Irene and Laura?" he said.

"It was great. Your friends are a lot of fun. Ed was a great partner, I can't believe we were on the same wave length. We should do it again. How about you?"

Boston's hands gripped the steering wheel tighter until his knuckles were white.

"Great," he said, through gritted teeth and she smiled to herself

She chattered on about the many funny things which happened over the course of the night and Boston's feelings of desire dissipated the more she spoke, especially about Ed's little quirks. By the time he reached her place, he was in no mood to be amorous at all.

"So are you staying the night?" she said.

"No, I'm too tired and have a lot of work to catch up on."

"Okay." She sounded disappointed and he felt bad. It wasn't her fault that her good time was a libido killer to him.

"How about we spend the day together tomorrow?"

"Great idea. Have a good night and I'll see you tomorrow." She leant over and gave him a quick kiss on the cheek.

He watched her go safely inside before heading back to his place. He thought tonight would be fun and it was, for her. He also planned to spend the rest of it making love to her, but now he simply had no desire.

Tomorrow he'd make up for tonight, he decided. Maybe tomorrow he'd even confess the truth.

Alyssa went inside relieved Boston didn't want sex tonight. Part of her was afraid if she let him touch her again, then she'd forget why she was doing all of this. She also couldn't avoid him because that would make him suspicious. Tomorrow, she was going to grill him about his past.

Chapter Fifteen

They were lazing under a tree after eating a delicious picnic lunch. Their hands entwined as Alyssa leaned back onto Boston knowing she was feeling a little too relaxed and happy. She needed to get her plan back on track before he seduced her into bed again, so she gave a loud sigh.

"What's wrong?" he said, as she knew he would.

Sitting up, she turned and looked at him.

"I'm frustrated I still can't remember you. Why is that?"

Boston sat up straighter and held her tightly.

"We'll make all new memories."

"But what happens if we have a fight and you bring up something I can't remember? Have we even had a fight yet? What was it about?" she said, despondent and he felt the heavy boulder of guilt on his shoulders.

"We haven't really had an argument yet. Things have gotten a little heated about how many ex-girlfriends I've had though." He lied about something plausible.

"Exactly my point. I don't remember," she said, sounding as frustrated as possible. "How many have you had?"

"Too many."

"Did you love *any* of them?"

"No." It was the truth.

"So you've never been tempted to get engaged and live the rest of your life with someone special?" she said, lifting head away from him so she could closely eye his reaction to the question.

"There was this one girl, Matilda or Mitzy as she was known. We were briefly engaged, but it didn't work out."

"Did you tell me this before?"

"No."

"Why not?"

"It's never come up."

"So you didn't love her even though you got engaged?"

"No, I think it was more a knee-jerk reaction to wanting what my sisters have," he said.

The Mitzy debacle was the most embarrassing and regretful moment in Boston's life that not even his siblings knew about. He put it down to a moment of madness upon seeing his two elder sisters so happy and in love. It was something he wanted and he had proposed to Mitzy without even really thinking it through. Luckily he quickly came to his senses and called it off before too many people knew.

"Wow, that's pretty impulsive. Do you think we'll get married one day?"

"Sure, why not?" he said, nonchalant, yet deep down knew he wanted Alyssa for his wife only he wasn't about to voice it, more because of his guilt at still lying to her.

"Gee, that sounds romantic," she said with slight sarcasm.

"Look, I don't know. We've only known each other a very short time," he said, frustrated, raking a hand through his hair.

"Exactly. You know all this *and I don't.*"

"Come on, Lys. It's not that bad."

She remained silent and refused to look at him.

Tell her! his brain screamed and yet, he remained silent. Then he looked at her and was about to ask something, which could ruin their day even more.

"Lys," he said, hesitant, as she just looked at him. "Why did you say that it was okay that Ed called you Ally when you told me you hate that name."

The emotions she felt through playing this charade were beginning to take a toll on her mind, yet she pushed on.

"We were just having fun and then you went all possessive."

"I wasn't being possessive," he said, half-hearted.

"*Right*," she said.

"But why didn't you tell him you didn't like being called Ally after I said it."

"It's one night. I think I'm a big enough girl to not care whether someone calls me by a nickname I do or don't like," she said, annoyed at him for bringing it up. While she might hate the name Ally, knowing Boston was a fake just made her dig her heels in about it.

"Fine. Next time I'll just keep my mouth shut."

"You do that," she snapped.

Her phone rang before he could say anything in reply and when she looked at it, she saw it was RB, the real Boston.

"It's my uncle. I'll be right back." She scrambled to answer it and made sure she was out of hearing distance before answering. RB was so funny and considerate. His timing even from overseas was perfect and strengthened her resolve to teach FB a lesson.

While she was talking, Boston sat there thinking about the situation. Like his family advised, he really needed to just come clean with Alyssa about the lie. Lord knows his lying to her made him feel even guiltier the more questions she asked. He could feel a simmering anger inside her and wondered if it would be better to have a fight over his lying and then they could start with a clean slate or put some distance between them. Yet somewhere deep down inside him, he was sceptical of his sisters' advice. He was worried they'd have the fight but never make up, which was why he was still trying hard not to confess. Unfortunately, his guilt was beginning to weigh heavier and heavier.

Looking at Alyssa on the phone, smiling and happy, made his stomach churn knowing he couldn't let her go.

She returned with renewed energy to grill Boston or at least try and trip him up.

"So how or why did you start your own company and what does it do?" she said, wondering what lies he would tell her. She could then compare that with the real Boston and hopefully tell fake Boston she'd caught him out.

"It's a *really* long story," he sighed.

"It's not like we don't have time so tell me, unless it's something really shady in which case, don't," she smiled.

He liked her teasing.

"Well, you asked for it…"

Boston was living with Indi and Jason in London. Montana and Lucas were frequent visitors. It was during one of those visits that Boston's life changed forever.

Around the table one morning after breakfast while Montana and Indi had gone off to hit the shops, he, Lucas and Jason were sitting reading the newspaper and talk turned to business.

"I see that the Kingston Group are heading for what we like to call, dun territory," Jason said.

"What does that mean?" Boston said, confused.

"It's an old English term and means the company is tanking. They're heading for bankruptcy."

"But I thought they had a big deal in the pipeline?" he said, curious as to what Jason would make of that.

"I hadn't heard anything about that," Jason frowned.

"It was in the paper about six or so months ago. Something to do with Scandinavia. I can't quite remember, a forest or resort?" he said, hesitant, hoping he wasn't making himself look like an idiot because he was mixing up businesses and news reports.

"I remember that," Lucas said. "They were linked to a company who run a lot of ski resorts and also own a lot of the forestry."

Lucas' comment just served to confirm Boston's memory was right on both accounts.

"Do you think the deal went ahead or not? It could explain why the paper says they aren't doing too well now?" Jason said.

Boston looked the Kingston Group up on the internet, amusing both Jason and Lucas.

"It says here they bought shares into the Nordic Hotel and Resort Group."

"Is there anything to give us a clue as to why they could be tanking?" Lucas said.

"Not really." Boston shook his head.

"I guess we'll just have to wait and see," Jason said.

"I wish I had the money to invest in the Kingston Group," Boston said.

"What?"

"Why?"

Both Jason and Lucas looked astounded by Boston's comment.

"Because I bet if you give them two years, they'll be back on top. There's a reason why they only bought shares into the Nordic Group and not the entire thing," he said.

"Maybe they just didn't have the capital," Lucas said.

"And you'd be throwing good money away," Jason said.

"I don't know. I just feel that if you can ride it out then it'll turn around," Boston said, puzzled that his gut instinct told him this company could be a winner.

Lucas and Jason shared a look that Boston missed as he was frowning at his laptop screen.

"Tell you what. Since you seem quite sure, Lucas and I will spot you some seed money to buy shares in the Kingston Group," Jason said.

The stunned look on Boston's face was a picture and the two men chuckled.

"You will? B-but what if it doesn't pan out? I-I mean, you just said that they're heading towards bankruptcy." Already he felt the pressure of this decision weighing heavily on him.

"Live and learn," Lucas said, with a dismissive wave of his hand. "We all have to start somewhere."

"And it wouldn't be the first time the newspaper's got

it wrong or is way behind the times," Jason smiled.

Boston couldn't believe his ears. These two men didn't have to lend him a cent, yet they were not only going to, but it was all because of his gut instinct. God, he hoped he was right, otherwise he'd be so ashamed. Even though he knew Jason and Lucas really didn't mind losing the money, still he didn't want to disappoint them.

"And while we may think it's not a good proposition, you think they're worth it," Lucas said.

"So, consider this your first real lesson," Jason said. "Trust your gut, knowing you possibly could be throwing away good money, or don't do it and sit on the sidelines waiting and seeing. Either way, Lucas and I will set you up with some money, that way if you have any more gut feelings, you can do something about it. Right, Lucas?"

"Right. It's a good idea," Lucas said.

"B-but what if I blow it all and prove I'm hopeless at investing?"

"Then you'll become our slave for ever," Lucas chuckled.

It turned out Boston's hunch had been a great one. Not only did the Kingston Group bounce back stronger than ever and in mere months, but it also made Boston wealthier. Offering his brothers-in-law their money back they told him to keep it.

Since that day, Boston began investing their money into different things he just felt were winners. While quite a few were, some were thankfully near misses and some were lessons to be learnt. But overall, Boston, Lucas and Jason, all realised Boston had a knack for smelling out great investment opportunities, which was why they decided to set him up with his own company, BC Corporation which took him to a whole new level of business.

While he had been happy to invest in companies, he realised he also wanted to own some outright, so he began doing that. Then he started buying companies before selling them onto others, all the while making sure to clip his ticket along the way.

Boston worked hard to make it a success and was even noted as someone to watch by some journalists.

To Boston it almost seemed like child's play knowing which companies to buy or invest in. He seemed to have a sense of connection with the people he did business with, knowing instinctively which people and companies would make him money. Because of his age, some thought to try and pull the wool over his eyes in the hope that Boston wouldn't realise.

Of course, Boston always made sure he did his due diligence. He wasn't one to just jump in, even if it seemed like a once in a lifetime opportunity was knocking. He also wasn't perturbed by a missed chance because of his thoroughness. He'd rather it just be a lost opportunity rather than a nightmare mess or loss he had to live with.

Thanks to both Lucas and Jason's guidance and unwavering support, they helped Boston become the success he was today. Yes, he had done all the hard work, but without his brothers-in-law great business acumen and mentoring he would have taken a lot longer to get to where he was, if he made it at all.

Now Boston was in news articles praising his meteoric rise and rags to riches story. Although some articles did also mention he was related to two wealthy families, Boston didn't mind because he openly acknowledged those family links and how grateful he was for them. He wasn't ashamed to have their support so if people wanted to call his success nepotism or a handout, let them. He knew the truth and to be honest, most people he dealt with were in the same boat as him. They too had affluent connections and didn't care as long as they were getting just as wealthy with him.

The even bigger mystery was how Boston managed to pick winners, which no one else seemed to even know about. To the even more experienced businessmen, Boston was just one of those lucky men who had great instinctive business nous.

"And that's how I got started. A little luck and help from my family," he said.

"Wow, you sound like a real boy wonder," Alyssa said, with an undertone of sarcasm that the story seemed so unbelievable she had to hand it to Boston for making it sound like he was just really fortunate. She wondered if he had gotten the money from some kind of scam or ill-gotten gains. Maybe that's what he did, he tried to scam rich women into giving him money. This just made her angry and her mood changed.

Things were awkward between them both until after dinner, then it became heated.

"Look, I don't know what's happening between us, but I feel like we're not quite on the same page at the moment," he said, confused because the day had been going so well and then all of a sudden Alyssa seemed to have changed and become angry at him for some unknown reason.

"Oh, you mean because I remember things except you," she snapped.

Alyssa was spoiling for a fight ever since she received a loving call from the real Boston, which made being with the fake one even more irritating.

"No, it's like you're a different person to…" He was going to say the one in the hospital, but stopped himself.

"To what?" She was beginning to yell. "To the one before she lost her memory? Or to the needy person from the hospital? Is that what you want? Someone needy so you can be the hero?" She was veering between anger and sarcasm.

"This is coming out all wrong." He dragged a hand through his hair.

She crossed her arms and stood there with a defiant look on her face and the words Avenging Angel came to mind. There was no doubt she was beautiful and he felt a powerful electrical charge go through him every time he saw her. More so the nearer he was to her, but since his trip away she was different. Had she remembered something or the lack of something?

"Have you remembered something about us, me?"

What, like the fact you're a big fat phoney, she wanted to sarcastically reply.

"Like what?" she said.

"I don't know," he said, frustrated. "I've got a business trip next week so I'll see you when I get back."

"You know what, don't bother."

Pain stabbed at him at her words.

"I'm tired of being your little girl lost. We're through."

He sighed and looked at her, his eyes sad as he just nodded and walked away, knowing this was all his own cowardly fault. He should have listened to his family and just told Alyssa the truth, but had been too chicken. Now he didn't have Alyssa at all and for once in his life, Boston actually felt his heart break. He also knew if he told her the truth now, there was no way she would ever believe it.

Chapter Sixteen

After Boston left, Alyssa felt her heart shatter and an uneasy sense that she didn't know who she was anymore. She should be jumping for joy; she had just dumped a lying con man, not crying her eyes out. Calling Claire and Liz to ask if they were free to catch up, Claire invited them to her house.

When she turned up, her long drawn face told the other two women just how bad the problem was. Hugging her tightly, they ushered her to sit and then explain, Claire with tissues on hand knowing Alyssa would need them.

"Okay, spill. What's happened?" Liz said, concerned.

"It's such a mess," Alyssa said, tears instantly falling. There was no holding them back.

"What is?" Claire said.

"My life. It all started with the accident," she said,

spilling the whole story out.

"I can't believe you had an accident and lost your memory and we didn't even know," Liz said, shaking her head once Alyssa finished speaking.

"I'm sorry, but I remembered you so I didn't think it was that important," she said.

"It's okay," Claire said.

"So you're saying you met a man named Boston Chan, the one we met at the club and then another man with the same name was pretending to be your boyfriend, only you didn't know until you saw the first Boston Chan and your memory came back?" Liz said, trying to sort out the confusion in her head.

"So there are *two* Boston Chans?" Claire said, stunned and Alyssa could only nod and wipe her eyes. "Holy moly, this is like a movie."

"How do you tell them apart? I'm completely confused," Liz said.

"One is RB, real Boston, the guy from the club and the other is FB, fake Boston, the guy from the hospital."

"Who also sounds like a total hottie," Claire said. "What? He does."

The other two women just looked at her.

"And you haven't seen much of RB?" Liz said.

"No, he seems to always be away on business, but he calls all the time."

"And now you've broken up with FB."

"Yes, because it was becoming so stressful pretending

I couldn't remember him, when I knew it's because he's not real. He's just a shameless imposter."

Liz and Claire looked at each other and silently exchanged understanding.

"What?" Alyssa said.

"Honey, are you sure RB *is* the real Boston?" Claire said. "He sounds like a fake."

"But I remember meeting him," she said.

"Okay, well how did the other Boston know you were in the hospital?" Liz said.

"Well, I did think he was joking when he said he randomly sat by unconscious female patients and since Uncle Jack was away on business and he…" She shrugged her shoulders having no answer as to how or why FB was at the hospital at all. "I have no idea," she sobbed, as the two women put their arms around her.

"And I hate to say it, but you seem awfully upset for someone who just kicked a lying jerk out of your life," Claire said.

"Have you asked Uncle Jack if he knows anything?" Liz said, when Alyssa finished crying,

"No, I was so busy being furious at being duped that I wanted to get back at him," she said, miserable.

"Oh, honey," Claire sympathised, hugging her again.

As soon as Uncle Jack arrived back in the country, Alyssa went to visit.

"How's my sunshine?" he said, enveloping her in a big hug.

"Great. How was your trip? How was Dad?" she said, to get the formalities out of the way, even though she still didn't remember her father.

"Fabulous. Those girls really know all about customer service and keeping the customer happy," he said, a twinkle in his eye as she screwed up her face at the thought. "Your father is well. A little bit greyer but well. He gave me something to give to you." He handed her an envelope.

Alyssa opened it up and took out the paper. As she looked at the bold penmanship on the paper, images began flying around in her mind of past letters swapped. Her head began to hurt and she closed her eyes, not noticing the photos which had fallen from the letter.

"Are you okay?" Jack said, instantly concerned at seeing Alyssa sway.

"Yes. I've got a bit of a headache, but at least now I remember my father or at least letters from him," she said, giving him a small smile.

"You remember…" he said, stunned. "What happened? I thought the doctor said you would be fine after the accident?"

"I am. Just had a few missing bits that's all. But they seem to have mostly come back to me."

"You didn't remember your father?" he said.

"No, but I guess that's probably more because I've

never met him and seeing his letter brought everything back to me," she said, to Jack's relief. Looking down at the floor she saw the old photos. "What's this?" She picked up the well-worn sepia photos. Seeing a picture of a happy couple holding their baby and then another one of them, but the baby was now a little girl. She burst into tears. It was the first time she had ever seen her father.

"W-why now?" she whispered.

"He found them a while ago and thought you might like them. They were the only photos he had of you."

Clutching them tightly to her chest, her eyes wet, she nodded.

"I'll treasure them always."

"So *are* you better from your accident?"

"I think so. Physically yes. Mentally, well, who knows, right?" she mocked. "Actually there's something I need to ask you about. Do you know why some strange man would just turn up at the hospital and pretend to be my boyfriend when I'm pretty sure I've never met him before. Memory or not."

"No idea," he said, as pink slashed his cheeks.

"Uncle Jack? What did you do?" she scolded.

"I was only thinking of you, Lys."

"What. Did. You. Do?"

"Thankfully you had just dumped that loser, Neil."

She definitely didn't need another reminder of what a jerk Neil was, she was more interested in her uncle's explanation.

"After your accident, your work called to tell me you were in the hospital. *They assured me you were fine*," he said, making sure she didn't think that he hadn't cared at all before he left on his trip. If the doctor had told him otherwise, he would have cancelled it.

"And?" It was like getting blood out of a stone and her patience was very quickly wearing thin.

"Since I was going to Hong Kong the next day, I went through your handbag to check nothing was stolen and I found a business card with Boston Chan's name on it."

Alyssa knew exactly which card he meant because it was what triggered this whole debacle.

"I don't know how you met him, but I figured he was a good guy and so I asked…"

She raised her eyebrow at him.

"Okay, *persuaded* the nurse to call him and say you, his girlfriend, were in an accident. If he asked, I was already out of the country and you had no one to look after you."

Her mind spun at Uncle Jack's explanation. She was now in turmoil because her uncle wanted her to hook up with some random man?

"But what if he had a girlfriend?"

"Then the nurse would have said she'd made a mistake. I'm sorry for meddling but believe me, a man like Boston Chan is worthy of you, Lys," he said, sincere.

"Do you even know him?"

"Only by reputation."

His answer didn't help. Did she tell her uncle what happened or not? Looking at him looking contrite and knowing she wasn't mad at him even if she wanted to throttle him at first, she sighed.

"You owe me."

"I'll make it up to you. What do you want?" He smiled, relieved and happy Alyssa wasn't mad.

"I'll think about it. Just be glad you're my uncle. Does Dad know?"

"Yes *and* he approved," he grinned.

"Well, he is better looking and younger than Stan Wong, I suppose," she giggled.

Admittedly relief flooded through her as Alyssa realised since Uncle Jack used the business card, obviously her initial thoughts were right about which man was the real Boston Chan and she was right to break up with the fake one.

Only there was now a very niggling sensation, one which really didn't make any sense. If Uncle Jack said he used Boston's business card, then why or how was it that the fake Boston was the one she woke up too? Was it possible that the fake Boston had overheard Uncle Jack and the nurse and saw this as some kind of opportunistic chance? And why hadn't the real Boston turned up at the hospital if he had been called? Unless the real Boston was away on business, which then gave the fake Boston a chance to put his con in motion. The real Boston also never mentioned being called or her being in the hospital.

The other uneasy question Alyssa had was the fact that the fake Boston didn't look at all nervous in the time they had been together. It was like he knew the real Boston was away. Perhaps that's what made him so believable, his confidence in his abilities.

Had he done this kind of thing before? The question then led her to wonder what was fake Boston's end game. What did he hope to achieve by trying to con her? Had he been like Neil and wanted to date her for her connection to Uncle Jack? Was he now hoping she regretted her decision enough to beg him to give her another chance, hooking her once more and using her guilt as leverage over her?

The real Boston, she shook her head knowing she didn't need to use that term anymore since there was now only one Boston in her life, she actually hadn't spent a lot of time with, other than the occasional dinner. She frowned at how was this relationship was going to survive if he was always working and never around. She was going to have to ask him about it the next time she saw him because she didn't want to just see him every other week, she wanted a real relationship, sort of like what she had with fake Boston.

Groaning to herself over her confusing and ridiculous thoughts, Alyssa wasn't sure which was more complex, losing bits of her memory or trying to sort out her love-life. At the moment it seemed her love-life was a lot harder.

Chapter Seventeen

Alyssa was excited when Boston called to say he was back in town earlier than expected and did she want to catch up for lunch. He named a fancy restaurant and she felt like she was being spoiled.

Her heart skipped a beat at seeing him again and at lunch they held hands or constantly touched both smiling like idiots to each other. Clearly she had been getting herself all worked up over nothing as the man sitting with her was the real deal.

"I bought you something," he grinned. "As soon as I saw it, I thought of you." A long black velvet jewellery case appeared on the table.

"Oh, you shouldn't have," she said, trying to contain her excitement as Boston's thoughtfulness made her feel all mushy and warm.

He opened the case and a lovely diamante bracelet was inside.

"It's beautiful." She smiled as he put it on her slender wrist and pulled her in for a kiss.

As she enjoyed their lunch, something niggled in the back of her mind as she remembered what she wanted to ask him.

"Hey, I was just wondering, what does your company do? Why did you decide to set it up, go into business for yourself?"

"A bit of this and a bit of that, really. It's not that exciting. Some wealthy men decided they saw some sort of genius in me and threw money my way to start me up," he said. "And, why talk about something so boring, when I'm having the most delicious lunch with you."

His hand stroked hers as his smile made her melt. This is what she liked about the real Boston, he was humble and clearly didn't feel the need to embellish his achievements unlike the over-the-top lie fake Boston made up.

"Do you have any siblings? Alyssa said.

"Yes, five," he said.

"Wow, that's a lot. I'm jealous. You must have a lot of great stories," she said.

"Not really. Anyway, let's not talk about something so boring."

His answers to her personal questions made her frown.

"I was wondering if you're free this weekend? I've

been so busy with work and thought a little time out would be perfect for the two of us to get away," he said.

How could she say no to him? A weekend away did sound idyllic. After all, this was exactly what she wanted and now she not only got her wish, but they would be able to discuss their future.

"Sounds perfect," she smiled.

"Oh and Ally, don't pack too many clothes," he grinned, giving her another quick kiss before turning and leaving.

Alyssa smiled to herself unable to believe she had finally found a boyfriend who not only made her smile, but also treated her like a princess.

Boston couldn't believe his eyes. He had broken up with Alyssa for barely a minute and there she was already lunching and kissing another man. As he watched the lovey-dovey couple come out of the restaurant and have a lingering goodbye, hurt and furious anger rose up inside him at what he thought of as her betrayal. He had been planning on coming clean with her, but instead she already had another boyfriend. Was that why she had been so different recently because she had been cheating on him? The thought boiled his blood and he wanted to go and punch that other guy's lights out.

"Alyssa. Lys."

Someone was calling her name and she looked around in her happy daze only to find the fake Boston approaching her.

"W-what are you doing here?" she said, her traitorous heart accelerating in excitement at seeing him as if it had forgotten they were broken up.

"Surprised to see me? I was surprised to see you having such a romantic lunch with another guy. It didn't take you long to move on," he said, his tone cool, glad they were in a quiet area so they could have some privacy.

"You saw me?" she gasped.

"So was he the reason why you'd been acting all weird? You were cheating on me?"

"Me? I'm not the one who's been lying," she said, her anger starting to rise.

"Tell me, when did you start seeing him? Have you slept with him?" he said, ignoring his guilt.

Her cheeks went pink answering for her.

"It's none of your business," she said.

"Is that from him? A lover's gift?" he said, looking at the bracelet on her wrist.

"It's *none* of your business. We're not together anymore," she snapped.

"It's cheap and tacky, not even real diamonds," he sneered.

"I don't care. At least he thinks of me."

"You think I don't, Lys?"

His tone quietened and made her anxious as his eyes

glistened with an intensity, which made her shiver.

"I think of you constantly. You're never not in my thoughts." He took a half step closer and hadn't let go of her wrist. In fact his thumb was rubbing it, distracting her from her anger.

"S-stay away from me," she said, taking a step backwards.

"Do you know what I'm always thinking?"

His husky timbre made her tremble and he could feel her pulse racing. His other hand moved up to the nape of her neck, holding her firmly but not hurting her, yet she couldn't do anything but look at him.

"This," he growled, before plundering her mouth.

She tried to push him away, but he held her tight making it so she felt his arousal, and knowing she too wanted what he could give her if she let him.

"Stop it! Stop it!" she said, wrenching herself free,

"Come now, Lys. We both want it. No one else is around, so your boyfriend won't even have to know."

His words and disgusting attitude made her burst into tears however, Boston refused to take the bait. Although after a minute he felt guilt swamp him and offered her his handkerchief.

"Thank you," she whispered, refusing to look at him and wondering why she hadn't yet left.

"So tell me, how long have you been seeing him?" His pride didn't want to know, yet there was a masochistic compulsion to hear the answer.

She didn't respond.

"Do you love him?" It choked him to have to ask and the hurt was unbearable agony.

"Why did you lie to me?" she said, looking at him tired and teary eyed with sadness in her eyes, ignoring his questions.

"Because we needed space. I didn't expect you to break up with me or go falling into the arms of the next available man you met." The underlying hurt and anger seeing her kiss another man, still simmered away inside him.

"*That's your excuse?* You lied to me because we needed space? You're still lying to me and can't even admit it," she said, furious.

"I don't know what you're talking about," he said, yet guilt stabbed at him, which he tried very hard to ignore.

Alyssa had never felt so angry in her life, not even about Neil or her father and she had been plenty mad about them.

"You don't *know* what I'm talking about? You don't know what I'm talking about?" she yelled, grateful there was no one walking past in the vicinity. "How about the fact *you have lied ever since you met me.* That's why *I* couldn't remember you because there was no you. You've pretended to be someone you're not and you have the nerve to accuse me of lying and cheating. *You, who is the epitome of a liar!*" she spat, seeing his face blanch at being caught out.

So she knew he lied.

"How long have you known?" he quietly said.

"Ever since you went away *for real*," she said, feeling lighter for getting it off her chest.

"How did you find out?"

"I called you."

Boston frowned and for an instant thought she was lying before flicking that away. There was no reason for her to lie, yet he knew he had never received a call from Alyssa while he was away.

"So all that other stuff since, was an act?" he said, trying to sort out everything in his mind.

"Oh no, you don't get to be the victim here. Do you know what it's like to lose your memory and have someone take advantage of that?" she said. "I wanted to know how far you'd go to lie to me. Well, I think I've proven you have no scruples at all. Even getting your friends to help you out. You disgust me."

"I have no idea what you're talking about."

"Sure, you don't. Just as I know you're not even Boston Chan, just some shameless impostor using another man's name."

The shock of her accusation felt like a hard slap to the face. Alyssa was accusing him of not being him while he was ashamed of the way he acted. He should have listened to his family and told her the truth. Being too chicken to do it he had lost her.

"Stay away from me. I never want to see you again,"

she said, pushing past him and running away, still wiping her eyes.

Boston was left reeling from Alyssa's accusation. If she didn't believe he was Boston Chan, then just who the hell did she think he was? His mind was such a befuddled mess he didn't even know where to begin to untangle his jumbled thoughts.

Alyssa was so shaken after her encounter with the fake Boston, she ditched work and went to see Uncle Jack. This was all his fault after all.

"Uncle Jack! Uncle Jack! Are you here?" She shouted at the top of her lungs in his house. His secretary said he was working from home this afternoon when she stopped by his office.

He came out of his bedroom with a robe on and she wasn't in the mood to give him any bantering about his hedonistic lifestyle.

"What's wrong, Lys? You normally call first," he said, concerned by her appearance.

"It's a mess, Uncle Jack," she said, holding back the tears.

"What is, honey?"

She looked at him closely and realised she had interrupted one of her uncle's daytime assignations, so she quickly turned away.

"Actually Uncle Jack, don't worry. I'll be fine. Just

having a panic attack over nothing. Sorry to interrupt," she said.

"Are you sure, Lys? You know you can tell me anything."

"I know. Go back to what you were doing. I need the girls."

"Lys, whatever it is, I'm always here and I'm sure it'll work out."

"I know and thanks. It means a lot."

Alyssa quickly left and called Claire and Liz. They'd know what to do.

Liz and Claire did know what to do. It involved a lot of junk food and more importantly a lot of tissues and sympathising.

"Do you feel any better?" Claire said, after Alyssa spilled the story of what had happened with both Bostons today to her friends.

"Not really," she mumbled.

"If it's any consolation, at least you got to tell the fake Boston you knew he was a no good liar. That must have felt good." Liz consoled.

"It did but…"

"But…" Her friends both said at the same time.

"Couldn't he have got down on his knees and begged and grovelled for my forgiveness?" she said, with a small smile making her friends laugh. "Or got all uppity and defensive so I could be absolutely furious, slap him and then storm off."

"He's a liar. A con man who clearly doesn't care he hurt you, Lys. You're better off firmly shutting the door. Besides, you've got a romantic weekend away with the real Boston." Liz heaved a dramatic sigh, making Alyssa smile.

"I remember those *long* ago days," Claire said, wistful. "Romantic getaways."

"Dirty weekends," Liz giggled.

"True. Thanks guys, I appreciate you coming over," she said.

"No worries, you would do the same for us," Claire said.

"Now did I tell you I interrupted Uncle Jack this afternoon and I don't think he was too pleased especially when I then turned around and left," she said.

They knew all about Uncle Jack's sex life and laughed at all the stories Alyssa would tell them.

Chapter Eightteen

After his accidental run-in with Alyssa, Boston was in the foulest possible mood and nothing could shake him from it. He was supposed to be negotiating a deal, but his mind just wasn't on business, it was on Alyssa and her wrongly flung accusations. He had never been told he wasn't himself before. His name was respected in the business world and yet, it stabbed him in the heart to know that Alyssa of all people called his character into question.

To her, he was a liar, and it was true. He had lied. There was no way he could ever regain her trust and knew he should have told her the truth from the very beginning.

His doorbell rang.

"Nix! What are you doing here? I thought you weren't arriving until next week?" he said, shocked, yet ecstatic to see his brother.

"Surprise! I was, but got an SOS from the states…"
The younger siblings nickname for their eldest sisters.
"Telling me I needed to leave a week early. Something
about you and *the one*, and you needed family and since
they couldn't make it, they thought I'd be the best one to
rescue you since I was already coming over. So here I am.
Of course, I made them upgrade me to First Class since
you know, I had them over a barrel," he chuckled.

Gripping Phoenix in a big bear hug, Boston didn't
even care about his older sisters' meddling. Just seeing
his brother right now was the best medicine he could have
ever received and the timing couldn't be more perfect.

"Since I'm now a week ahead of my plans, my *rich*
older brother is going to have to pay for everything,
otherwise I'll be flat broke by the time I get to London,"
Phoenix grinned. "I tell you, I wish everyone was this
desperate all the time, I could get used to living like a
king."

"Like you won't be mooching off Indi in London,"
Boston grinned, still unable to believe his brother was
here, standing in front of him.

"True," Phoenix smiled, then turned sober. "So tell me
about this woman that's made you all sad and miserable.
I barely know a thing."

"It's a *long* story," he sighed.

"Which is why I'm a week ahead of schedule. Now
you have all the time in the world to explain it to me."

"It's very confusing."

"After the states' love stories, when is it not," Phoenix chuckled. "So can you top them?"

"I'm not sure. Possibly, or its at least on par with them?"

"Great, now I can't wait to hear all about it," Phoenix smiled. "Let me just get comfy. Okay, lay it on me."

Boston smiled. It really was great having his brother here. However, after he explained as much as he could, even Phoenix was confused.

"You're sure she accused you of not being *you*? That's just bizarre."

"That's what I think too. Just who does she think I am?" he said.

"Well, why don't you tell me how to find her and I'll say I'm you, after all, we're not only brothers, but look similar," Phoenix teased.

That caused Boston to scowl at the thought of his own brother hitting on Alyssa.

"No way. You're not ever going *near* her."

"Boy, you are so into this woman," Phoenix laughed. "I don't think you'd have cared if I made a move on any of your past girlfriends. Not that I have."

"That's right, and let's keep it that way," he growled.

"Actually, Alyssa's given me a great idea. I'm going to use your name when I'm out and about and see how many ladies I can pull," Phoenix said, waggling his eyebrows.

"Don't you dare. I don't need my hard-earned reputation tossed down the drain by your antics."

"Fine." Phoenix heaved a dramatic sigh, then grinned. "I'll just tell them the truth, that I'm the younger, hotter, way more sexier brother."

Boston couldn't help but laugh. Yes, it was good to have Phoenix here.

The two brothers spent the next few weeks enjoying their catch up and just when Boston almost felt back to normal again, it was time for Phoenix to move onto London as planned.

"I'll miss this," Boston sighed.

"Me too. I missed it when you left, but I guess this time I'm the one leaving."

"Yes, but at least it's a quick plane ride and I'm over there often so we'll see each other more."

"I hope so. Love you, Bos."

"Love you, Nix."

They embraced knowing their brotherly bond was still just as strong as ever.

Boston was deflated now Phoenix had left and he was no further in getting over Alyssa. Trying to keep his mind off her, he was currently being distracted by attending his friend, Paul Akerman's company golf day. Even though he wasn't really in the mood to mingle, for his friend he was willing to put in an appearance. He knew his attendance would help Paul's career and he could also theoretically do some networking.

At the clubhouse, he wandered around chatting and mingling with Paul's bosses who were happily surprised Boston was only in attendance because he knew Paul. Boston knew they were now looking at his friend in a whole new light.

"Oh my God, did you see who Paul managed to get to attend today?" one man said, to the group he was standing in.

"Who?"

"Boston Chan."

Boston overheard the conversation and smiled to himself.

"Who's that?" a man said.

"How do you not know who Boston Chan is? He's been in the papers. You know, one of those 'self-made' men who had the backing of some wealthy relations to help him get started, but has since become a success."

"Oh, that guy. He's mega rich now. They say his company is worth millions."

"And Paul knows him?"

"Yes, Paul said they're friends and Boston was doing him a favour showing up today, lucky dog," one man said, envious.

"I'll say. I wondered how Paul got put into a group with some of the senior execs."

"What are you boys talking about?" a man said, approaching the group.

"Hey Neil, you finally finished your round. How'd it go?"

"What a bore," he moaned. "They stuck me with some of the other office losers. How am I supposed to schmooze the bosses with them?"

"Well, you can try now?"

"Doubt it. Having their almost undivided attention for the course meant I could have really pushed how awesome I am. Now I have to fight everyone else for their attention."

"You should have done what Paul did."

"What's that?"

"Get a big shot to attend."

"He's pulled a page out of my playbook," Neil said, jealous and to confused looks on the other men's faces before explaining about his cheating exploits with Alyssa. "So you wouldn't believe who her uncle is, Jack Lee."

"Who?" someone said.

"Jack Lee. He owns a lot of businesses all over the city like The Flamingo Palace."

"Oh wow."

"I know. So I'm thinking if I could make it known I'm dating Jack's niece, then upstairs will put me on the fast track, so I go spouting off at work about her and him, right?"

"What about your girlfriend, Ally?" one of the men said, eager to hear more.

"Oh, she was totally cool with it. Totally understood I

wasn't into the niece, as hot as she was, so she was happy to let me play the field," Neil crowed, as the rest of the men in the group looked green with envy his girlfriend was happy to let him cheat on her. "Although between you and me, if she wanted me to marry her, I'd have done it just to be Jack's nephew-in-law. Imagine the clout I'd have."

The men hanging on to the Neil's every word could only nod.

"Where was I? Oh yeah, so upstairs seemed into it, but then interest fades so I needed to shove it in their faces because there was a chance of promotion as one of the senior execs just resigned. I organise this *huge* fancy party, I say for my birthday and then the bitch decides to dump me right before it," he said, furious.

"Why?"

"All because I went behind her back to precious uncle and invited him. I knew she wasn't going to ask him even though she said she would."

"Then what happened?"

"I panicked. Pretended to grovel and the bitch pretended to accept my apology and then ditches me on the night so I'm left looking like a schmuck to everyone."

"Wow, that's cold," one of the men sympathised.

"I know. What a bitch, right? Just because she's a looker and has got a rich uncle doesn't mean squat." He wallowed in self-pity.

"Did you get the promotion?"

"Are you kidding? When they realised Jack wasn't coming, it was over. That's why I had to leave the company."

"I guess I probably would have done the same."

Heads nodded in agreement.

"I got the last laugh though. Every time I banged her and called her Ally, I was thinking of my Ally, not her," Neil derisively laughed.

Boston's fists clenched tightly at what he'd just over-heard, disgusted by some man's attempt to get ahead by using some poor woman.

He didn't make himself known to the men, but instead moved so he could see their faces from afar. To his surprise, one of the men was the same man Sam pointed out to him the day he first saw Alyssa. No wonder she hated the name Ally. Now it all made sense.

What did that jerk say Alyssa's uncle's name was again? Jack. Jack Lee. Boston laughed to himself. He knew a Jack Lee by reputation only and could only hope the Jack Lee he was thinking of was Alyssa's uncle.

Deciding to be proactive and take the bull by the horns, Boston was going to see 'uncle' Jack and hope he could shed some light on the situation.

Jack was in his office waiting in excited anticipation for his meeting with Boston Chan. He couldn't stop himself from smiling about his cunning plan until Alyssa caught him out. He wondered if they were dating and knew it was probably way too much to hope after such a short period of time, Boston would be coming to ask for Alyssa's hand in marriage. Still, dreams were free.

He frowned remembering how upset Alyssa had been the other day and since that afternoon had seen neither hide nor hair of her. Although they talked on the phone, he had a feeling she was avoiding him for some strange reason, and as tempted as he was to get one of his investigators to discreetly check up on her, the guilt over his little trick surfaced so he left her alone hoping she would soon come and talk to him and explain what's going on with her.

"Boston. Come in and sit down," he said, shaking his hand and ushering him to a seat. "What can I do for you? To be honest, I was surprised you wanted a meeting."

They didn't move in the same business circles so Boston knew Jack had to be curious about this meeting.

They talked about inconsequential things until the coffee came and once they were alone, Boston cut to the chase.

"Jack, am I right in guessing that Alyssa Lee is your niece?" he said.

"Why yes, here's her photo?" Jack said, puzzled as he held up a frame for Boston to see his beautiful niece's smiling face.

"And while you were out of town, Alyssa had an accident and for some strange reason, and I have racked my brain, but for the life of me can't figure out why I was called as her next of kin."

Jack's cheeks went pink as he shifted uncomfortably in his chair. So Boston was angry at his little set-up and while the wise course of action was to say nothing, instead he spoke.

"What exactly are you after?" Jack said. "Revenge? Payback? What? Alyssa had nothing to do with it."

Boston just looked at him. So Jack did know how all this came about.

"No, I just need to understand, why me?" He saw the relief flood through the older man at his question.

"Maybe you met her earlier and she mumbled your name in her sleep?" Jack said, hope threaded through his voice.

Boston shook his head. Even though he had never actually met Alyssa before the hospital, it didn't mean she couldn't know his name, yet if that were the case, then why would she think he wasn't him? That was the part confusing him the most.

Jack knew he should confess his part in this to the younger man sitting opposite him, but first he wanted to take a punt on a hunch he had.

"If you're not here for payback and want to understand, I'm guessing you and Lys are dating or dated?" he said, trying hard to squash down his excitement.

"I'm not sure you could call it that," he sighed. "But that was after the whole hospital mix-up."

"Maybe it wasn't a mix-up at all. Maybe you were meant to be called."

"That's why I'm here. I really don't understand, why call me? It wasn't as if I knew her. It's like someone just picked a random name out of thin air which just happened to be mine."

Now Jack was confused. Alyssa had Boston's business card and yet, here was Boston claiming he'd never met her. It was time to show his cards and hope it still was a winning hand.

"I confess it was my doing. It had nothing to do with Lyssa."

"You? Why?" Boston said, shocked.

"Because of Lyssa's very bad run of men and I wanted to help her," Jack said. "The hospital called me to say she had an accident so I went and checked on her. While I was there I found your business card in her handbag and assumed she met you, so I organised for the hospital to contact you pretending Lys was your girlfriend. If you had a girlfriend, they'd say they made a mistake."

"Whoa, whoa. *You* did this? You set me up because your niece has bad luck picking men?" he said, incredulous, anger and irritation flowing out of him knowing he had been played by both uncle and niece.

"I'm sorry, but you're the kind of man I wanted Lys dating. You can take it out on me, but don't take it out on her. *She didn't know.*"

The pleading in Jack's voice made Boston soften

slightly however, he still had so many unanswered questions.

"You say you found *my* business card in her wallet, but I'd never met her." The confusion in his voice evident.

"What can I say? Maybe she got it from someone at your firm."

Boston pondered Jack's reasoning. There was logic to it yet, it still didn't seem to make any kind of sense.

"Thanks for your time," he said, shaking Jack's hand.

"No problem. I'm sorry for playing a terrible trick which obviously back fired on you and Lys. I had hoped…"

"I know and it's not entirely your fault."

Boston left Jack's office deep in thought. Alyssa claimed he wasn't Boston Chan, but an impostor. Jack said he found Boston's business card and assumed they'd met. If they had met socially, there was no way he would have given her his business card. He would have made sure she programmed his numbers into her phone. So how did she get his business card? Then another thought hit. Alyssa said she called him, but he never received a call from her because he would have answered. So just who were the Lee family calling? Were they being scammed and didn't know it? All these thoughts left him even more confused than ever.

Chapter Nineteen

As Alyssa packed a weekend bag to take to work as the real Boston said he'd pick her up to leave from there, she was repeatedly telling herself she was excited about their weekend away. Alyssa was proud of how she confronted the fake Boston with the truth. Now that he knew she knew he was a liar, he'd never bother her again. Something she was happy about, even though she was also trying very hard to ignore the ache in her heart.

Now as she came out of the elevator she saw the fake Boston's friend, Sam getting a coffee from the coffee stall in the foyer. He looked up, saw her and smiled.

"Hi Alyssa, how are you?" he said.

"I'm fine, thanks," she said, annoyed he saw her and therefore couldn't avoid him. "How are you?"

"Good, thanks," he grinned, noting she was carrying

a bag. "Going away for the weekend with Boston, huh?"

"Yes. How did…" She looked perplexed by his comment, then saw Boston outside coming towards them and quickly said, "I have to go. Have a nice weekend."

"You too." Waiting for the elevator Sam saw Alyssa kissing Boston and grinned until he realised the man wasn't Boston, but someone else.

In the elevator ride back up to his office Sam wondered if Alyssa lied on purpose and should he tell his friend? Or maybe they had broken up and she hadn't wanted to answer any awkward questions. Deciding it was best to stay out of it, he packed his briefcase and went home.

Boston went over to Alyssa's and loudly banged on her door. He was tired of his mind going round in circles with no end in sight. He was just going to ask her where she got his business card from, certain it was the key to this whole mess and then he could go back to resuming his uncomplicated carefree lifestyle.

He kept banging until he realised she wasn't home. Where could she be? Was she with *him*, the guy she had lunch with? The thought ate away at him and deciding he needed some sort of distraction, he went out clubbing with friends and met a blonde who was eating him alive with her eyes, which was always a good sign.

"Can I buy you a drink?" he said, as she brazenly pushed herself onto him and kissed him.

Taken aback by her forwardness, he then went with the flow until they broke apart and she grinned.

"Let's find somewhere *a lot* quieter," she said.

Who was he to say no? She dragged him outside so they could find a taxi.

"I'm Michelle Hanlon," she said.

"Boston Chan."

"Oh man, seriously?" she whined. "How many of you are there?"

"Excuse me?" he said, confused by her reaction to his name.

"Look, guy," she said, irritated this hot guy was playing her. "I've already run into one of you last night. I don't need another one."

"I don't know what you're talking about," he said, bewildered.

She sighed, knowing this guy was taking the charade seriously so she decided to just tell him the honest truth to his face.

"Look, I don't know whose great idea this was, but now there's too many of you. You need to get a new name. Or better yet, use your own name. You're hot enough that you'd still get laid. There's no need to pretend," Michelle said.

His mind spun in a million different directions at what this woman in front of him was trying to tell him.

"Okay, I'm confused. My name's Boston —"

"Chan. I know. Like I said, I met one of you last night."

"What do you mean, you met one of me?"

"You're really playing this to the hilt. Well, that's a first. Normally you guys don't try so hard. Once you get busted you just move on to the next unsuspecting woman who hopefully hasn't been warned about you," she shrugged.

"Again, what did you mean by 'one of me'?"

"As if you don't know," she sighed. "Fine, I'll explain. There's a whole bunch of you pretending to be Boston Chan. You hit on girls for one-night stands, give them your card to impress them and then if anyone calls, you juggle or ditch them," she said, exasperated. "Like I said, use your own name or at least find another fake name."

"But *I am* Boston Chan."

Michelle snorted her disbelief.

"Thanks for your help," he said, leaving her to go back inside while he went home as everything was now becoming very clear to him.

The reason Alyssa thought he was a fake since she didn't remember him was because she must have met and remembered a fake Boston Chan. How ironic that without her losing her memory, he would never have known men were using his name to get laid. Should he be flattered or annoyed? After all, it was pretty ingenious except it was his name and reputation they were all ruining.

Frustration shot through him when he went around to Alyssa's and she wasn't home. He didn't want to call her and talk, as this was something that needed to be done face to face. In the end he called Jack, deciding it might be more helpful to get some more clarification before approaching Alyssa again.

Jack was not only surprised to hear from Boston again, but invited him over to the house.

Boston was stunned and embarrassed to see topless women cavorting openly in front of him.

"Ah, should I come back?" he said, hesitant as Jack roared with laughter.

"No, they're my distractions. Stress-relief if you will."

"Uh-huh." He was feeling very uncomfortable and realised Alyssa's description of her uncle was heavily diluted.

"Now what's this all about?" Jack was surprised to get another call from Boston after their last encounter.

Jack noticing Boston couldn't think straight with all the female distractions going on, ushered him into his office.

"Okay, what brings you by?"

"I have a couple of questions for you."

"Shoot."

"You said that you found *my* business card in Lyssa's wallet," he said. "You also said you got the hospital to call me."

Jack nodded again thinking this was all old ground that they had covered last time.

"Did you give the hospital the card to call me?" he said, hoping for the answer he suspected.

"No. I just asked Nurse Gilmour to call Boston Chan at BC Investments. Why?" Now Jack was curious. Why did it matter whether he gave the hospital the card or not?

"Because that's why they rang me and not the other Boston," he smiled, pulling out his wallet and a card. "And just to confirm, this wasn't the card you saw in Lyssa's wallet, was it?"

Jack didn't have any idea what was going on, but as soon as he saw the card Boston handed him, he knew it wasn't the same as the one he saw.

"No. Are you going to explain about this *other* Boston?" Jack said.

"It's a long story, which now makes so much more sense." Seeing Jack's bewildered face, Boston realised he was speaking cryptically. "Let's just say I've recently discovered there are men impersonating me at nightclubs. I don't suppose you know where Alyssa is, do you?"

"No. All I know is that she went away for the weekend. I'm very confused, but good luck," Jack said, nonplussed, yet smiling.

After Boston left, Jack was pretty sure the next time he saw him, it would be announced he was going to be his future nephew-in-law and that was something Jack could easily stomach. To celebrate, he went out to continue cavorting with his bevy of beauties.

Phoenix, Jason and Lucas were all in town for a boys' weekend they said. It was unspoken they were all here to check up on Boston and it showed just how worried they were that even Jason, who was loathed to be parted even a minute from his newborn son, came. It helped that Montana was with Indi so Jason was more relaxed about the weekend.

For Boston, their timing couldn't have been better. He was miserable and needed his family to help cheer him up or at least give him the support he needed.

"Okay, so the last thing we heard according to Nix's retelling of the story, is Alyssa thought that you weren't you," Lucas said.

"Yes, can you tell us again what happened, because it was a little confusing. Perhaps something got lost in translation?" Jason said, teasing Phoenix.

"That's just because it's clearly too complicated for you and you're not smart enough to follow it," Phoenix grinned. "Just ignore him, Bos. He's got baby brain and unless it's about Christopher, he's not listening."

"Too true," Jason smiled, checking his phone to see if Indi had texted him any updates.

"Good grief," Lucas teased. "Christopher won't grow up that quick."

"You tell me you weren't like this with any of your children," Jason said.

"Of course not. I was too busy fending off my own family and Mon's best friends who were hogging the baby to even get any kind of alone time with my own child," Lucas laughed. "You know that there's something about a baby that just calls to everyone, whether it's your first or tenth."

"So true," Jason chuckled. "But seriously Bos, can you do a recap?"

"Why not? It's a long story. One that really has to be seen or lived to be believed," he sighed. "I've only just found out this new piece of the puzzle the other night, which is probably the most important piece. I'm not sure if this con is done in the UK, but it seems that men do it here. Apparently, men impersonate famous or wealthy men in nightclubs to try and score women. They even have business cards made up so it looks legit."

"Wow." Everyone's eyes boggled.

"The women are generally none the wiser it's a con. I think as long as you look similar you could probably pull it off, or find someone who just has no idea what the man being impersonated looks like or any details of their lives other than their name," Boston said.

"So, there's men out there impersonating you," Lucas said, rubbing his chin.

"Apparently. I only found out when I went clubbing and told a woman my name. She started telling me to stop lying about being me, that she had already met 'one of me' before. Believe me, I was so confused even I had to get her to explain it to *me*."

"Wow, now I can see how it would be like speaking in riddles to each other. So you gave her your card?" Jason said.

"No, she probably still wouldn't have believed me anyway. She's the one who told me the fake Bostons also have business cards."

"So how does Alyssa fit into all this?" Lucas said, having already put all the pieces together, yet still wanting to hear it from his brother-in-law.

"Like I said, it's so convoluted and mind-boggling. Alyssa was knocked down by a mugger and was in the hospital. I was called as her 'boyfriend' and obviously, since I didn't have a girlfriend or recognise the name, I still went just in case I knew who she was and could help contact her family or any friends on her behalf," he said.

The three men nodded their agreement knowing they would have done the same thing.

"When I saw her, I was shocked, it turned out that Alyssa was my mystery woman who I had seen one day when I was with my friend, Sam in his building lobby."

"Whoa. What? What mystery woman? You never mentioned this the first time you told me about her," Phoenix said. "You only said the hospital called."

Boston felt guilty he hadn't told his brother about his initial reaction to Alyssa.

"Sorry Nix. The first time I saw Alyssa she was coming out of the elevator and I swear that the whole world disappeared and there was only the two of us in it. It even felt like we had a telepathic conversation."

Phoenix stared at his brother while his face looked gobsmacked by his confession.

"Oh my God. I… Wow," was all Phoenix could say.

"Alyssa truly is your *one*," Jason smiled.

"Definitely," Lucas nodded. "And thank God you never told your sisters this bit."

"I agree," Jason said. "If you had told your sisters this, they'd have been over here in a shot introducing themselves to Alyssa and welcoming her into the family. Making sure she had no choice, but to end up with you."

"That's true," Lucas chuckled.

Boston silently agreed with his brothers-in-law. If he had told his sisters, they would have done what Jason just said. It may have also saved him a world of heartache and confusion.

"So tell us how the truth came out," Lucas said.

"So while Alyssa might have had amnesia, she was regaining her memory quite quickly. Only, of course, in relation to me, I was still a big blank in her mind. Believe me it was hard to act like we had any kind of history when it was non-existent. Fudging the truth was hard and made me feel guilty every time."

"So, you didn't take everyone's advice to tell her the truth," Lucas said.

"I couldn't," Boston said, annoyed Lucas reminded him of his stupidity.

"I wouldn't have either," Lucas said.

"Me either," Jason said.

"You guys wouldn't have?" Boston said, surprised. "But you were the ones who told me to."

"Because now in all our worldly wisdom and being spectators, as we said at the time, it's easier to give advice than to actually take it," Lucas said.

"So true. If I was in your position, I still would be fudging the truth hoping she never finds out. No one wants to own up to the fact that you've been lying to the person you love," Jason said.

"Thank God, I'm not even close to having these problems," Phoenix chuckled, lightening the mood.

"You wait. It's your turn next," Jason teased.

"Whatever. I'm not going to be getting myself tied up into knots all over some woman."

"Famous last words, Nix," Lucas laughed.

"I agree, Nix. When love hits, I bet you'll be running around like a headless chicken. Learn from us, honesty is the best policy," Boston said.

"You guys just said you wouldn't take your own advice," Phoenix said.

"Which is why you should. Make it easier on yourself," Jason said.

"Anyway, back to the story," Phoenix said, not wanting to listen to more pearls of wisdom. There was no way he would be in this kind of pickle when he finally found the woman of his dreams, which was certain to be many years away.

"Yes, so how did she find out you weren't you, or that there was another guy running around pretending to be you, which she thought was the real you?" Jason said, still looking slightly confused as did the others.

"It all happened when I came to visit you and meet Christopher. Something triggered her memory and she realised the 'Boston' she remembered wasn't me, thus accusing me of being a fake and conning her," he said. "I tried to explain, but because I hadn't been truthful from the beginning she didn't believe me."

"Okay, so now we're pretty much up to speed. So why did the hospital call you and not the other Boston?" Lucas said.

"Well, that was one of the things I couldn't quite understand. None of this would have happened if the hospital had called the other Boston," he said. "Recently I was at a golf day for a friend and overheard this guy talking about cheating on his girlfriend, with her approval—"

"What?"

"No way."

"Wow."

Boston smiled at the three reactions.

"It turns out the man was Alyssa ex-boyfriend who my friend, Sam pointed out to me the first time I saw Alyssa. It seems her ex was using Alyssa to try and get a promotion because her uncle was Jack Lee, someone connected enough in business circles over here."

"Bastard," Phoenix hissed.

"I agree," Jason said, as Lucas nodded.

"I went and visited Jack to see if he was indeed Alyssa's uncle. It turned out not only was he, but he was the one who persuaded the nurse at the hospital to call me on the pretext that he was out of town and I was her boyfriend. The mix up happened because the nurse called me using the directory and not the business card Alyssa had on her, otherwise the nurse would have called the other Boston."

"Well, that's one complicated and messy story, but if that's not fate, then I don't know what is," Lucas smiled.

"I agree. The universe clearly wants you both to be together," Jason chuckled.

"So Alyssa still doesn't realise the the other guy is a fake?" Phoenix said.

"I don't think so," Boston said, with a sad shake of his head.

"Nix, you've been clubbing and raving in London. Are men using the same con?" Lucas said.

"No idea," he shrugged, then chuckled. "But I have asked Bos if I can use his name. At least he knows me and let's face it, we look similar enough that even if anyone suspected I wasn't him, I could still answer enough questions to be him."

Lucas and Jason both chuckled at their brother-in-law's cheekiness as Boston still didn't look impressed by his brother doing anything along those lines.

"So now what?" Jason said. "Have you seen Alyssa?"

"Unfortunately yes. I saw her and some new guy at lunch, which was when she accused me of not being me. And now that I've managed to untangle a few of the crossed wires, I've tried to get hold of her, but she's not home and it's not something I want to discuss over the phone."

All the men in the room were nodding their heads. This was definitely a discussion to be had in person.

"Not to worry, Bos. Not only do we all have your back, we know that you'll end up together. After all, the universe has spoken," Lucas smiled.

"I hope so," he said.

Chapter Twenty

Alyssa should have known this weekend wasn't going to go according to plan when Boston turned up in a car she hadn't expected at all. After his explanation that he swapped cars with a friend who not only needed something bigger, but was also trying to impress a woman, she couldn't help but think that Boston was such a nice guy and a great friend.

Since they were all alone and there wasn't much to do except talk, she decided to ask him the question that had been niggling her.

"Why didn't you come to the hospital?" she said.

"What's that, babe?"

"Why didn't you come to the hospital when they called?"

"Honestly, life has been so hectic since we met that I

don't even know which way is up half the time. Besides, I've been away for work quite a lot which was why I couldn't come, otherwise I'd have been there for sure," he said, grabbing her hand and kissing it.

After hearing his explanation, Alyssa felt foolish for even doubting the reason. Although she had to squash down thoughts of how he didn't even seem interested in what happened at the hospital. Ever since she had re-connected with Boston, he had constantly been away on business, which made this weekend even more special.

Only now she was miserable. First their car broke down along the back road in the middle of nowhere and then Boston left her all alone to get help with a random passerby who kindly stopped to help. Since there was only room for one other person in her tiny little car, Boston said he would go and wouldn't be long. The woman looked delighted to take Boston, and he seemed just as happy with the arrangement.

Sitting there and out of sheer boredom, Alyssa began snooping through the glove compartment of the car without an ounce of guilt. It was pretty icky at first glance with chocolate bar wrappers and other rubbish. She hadn't expected Boston's friend to be so gross. As she continued to rummage, her eyes caught on an old faded Polaroid which read on the back: *To Keith, this is all for you xxx.* Even though the picture was very faded, it was obvious the woman was naked. It seemed that Boston's friend, Keith was just plain disgusting.

Then she went through every other compartment in the car to help pass the time and found Boston's wallet in the middle console, which he had forgotten to take with him. Flicking through it seemed like an invasion of privacy, but since he had just left her, she felt justified in snooping. Shock rumbled through her as his driver's license read Keith Wong and yet, the photo was undeniably of Boston. Alyssa blinked, then blinked again thinking there had to be some kind of mistake. However, all the various cards including bank cards were also for Keith Wong before she then found tucked inside, the same white cards as the one he had given her on that first night which read: Boston Chan.

Alyssa's world spun off its axis at the realisation. She had been conned by the fake Boston into thinking he was the real one. She wanted to be sick, yet somehow managed to remain calm.

Since there was nothing else to do, she decided to definitely breach more of his privacy and unashamedly went through his weekend bag only to find another cell phone. She also found a video camera and turned it on to look at the contents.

There were screeds of footage of him and different women having sex. Deleting it all in a fit of disgust and anger, she put it back and sat in the car thinking about what she was going to do, all the while kicking herself for having been so stupid as to be taken in by this man. Sighing she knew this was all because of her memory loss. If it hadn't happened, would she have ever met the real Boston Chan and would this Boston have kept stringing her along with her being none the wiser. Would she have ever found out the truth?

It was only luck their car broke down and she found his wallet, otherwise she would have still believed Keith was Boston. This then led her to thoughts of how many other women had he done or was doing this too? Was she the only idiot or were there more unsuspecting women out there? Were those the ones on his video camera? The thought made her even angrier at Keith's treachery.

Finally, Boston/Keith returned with a tow truck however, his shirt was all askew and she instantly knew he'd had sex with the blonde Samaritan. As disgusted as Alyssa was, sadly she somehow found it unsurprising now she knew what a deceitful, lying creep he really was.

"There's a motel a few miles from here where Dave's going to drop us off so we can at least be comfy for the night," Keith said, and she simply nodded her agreement.

In the town, Dave kindly dropped them off at an open garage and as Alyssa looked around, she saw a rental car place. Hallelujah! she wanted to shout and while Keith was sorting out the car with the mechanic, she walked there, hired a car and began driving back home.

Keith called frantically looking for her when she finally relented and answered.

"Where are you? I thought we were having a romantic weekend?" he said, anxious.

"You can keep the buxom blonde."

"*It was a lift.*"

"I bet. Your clothes tell a different story." The pause on the line told her he was looking down at his clothes. "Oh, and Keith?"

"Yes," he said, before swearing.

Alyssa disconnected the call and laughed out loud to herself before her thoughts turned to misery. She had thrown away a great man all for a stupid illusion.

Driving while distracted wasn't a good thing at the best of times however Alyssa couldn't help herself. Alone with tons of time on her hands, her mind kept wandering back to the two Bostons.

The man who she now knew was the *real* Boston, who had lied and yet, still took care of her. Never once had he pressured her into anything she wasn't willing to do. Why hadn't he just left her at the hospital to her own devices? Just said, "I have no idea who she is," and left. Or even after he kindly saw her home, told her the truth and left. What made someone like him, someone who was a very busy man, a self-confessed workaholic, stop his life just for her? Not once in all the time she knew him had he ever put work first. In fact, if she was being truthful to herself, she could have sworn he put her — a total stranger — first.

Yes, there was chemistry between them, nevertheless he still could have just popped in and out or rang and checked on her if he was concerned. He hadn't needed to have stayed especially since he kept to his word to not pressure her into sleeping with him.

Then there was the other, *fake* Boston, who she now knew was actually Keith Wong. How could she not have seen just how fake he was? Admittedly, her faulty memory was partly to blame, yet even then she hadn't felt the same strong attraction to him.

Now she knew why he was always away on 'business'. He clearly was just using the time to juggle women. More for sex, if his video camera was to be believed, rather than actually wanting to be in a relationship with them. She knew if she truly wanted a relationship and to talk about their future, he would have either kept trying to string her along or this weekend would have just been one for the road as they parted ways, probably with him saying he was too busy to be tied down or some other excuse.

It also made his vague answers to her personal questions more understandable.

So why hadn't she just cut her losses with both Bostons? That was the question she really didn't want to answer and therefore hoped to ignore it for as long as possible. What she did know was that it definitely wasn't because she was on the rebound from Neil.

Once again, her thoughts drifted to the real Boston. He said he saw her in the building foyer one day with a friend, who she now knew to be Sam. Yet, that was the only time he had ever seen her until the hospital. Had anything he said during their week together even been the truth? The stories he told about his family? Was any of it true?

Home sweet home! She was going to crawl into bed and never get out. Her head ached full of memories and confusion. At least now she practically remembered everything about her life except for the actual accident. From that day all she remembered was walking to the deli and then waking up in the hospital.

Closing her eyes, sleep came quickly.

Waking and noting the time on her clock read ten in the morning, she purposely spent the weekend by herself just blobbing and relaxing, ignoring all phone calls as if she really were away. So much had happened and she really needed time to get her head around it all and reflect on the chaos created.

This introspection needed to start with Neil. A complete moron and a man she should never have dated. However, he was the last and sadly just one in a very long string of losers who weren't right for her.

Then there was the interfering absentee father with good intentions sending her *old* or should that be decrepit Stan Wong, even if it had been a mistaken identity mix-up.

And what about her well-meaning interfering uncle who sent her a fake boyfriend who just so happened to have an impersonator running around causing chaos and who she ironically just happened to meet before she meets the real deal.

Next was Boston Chan. The real Boston Chan. The man she accused of being an impostor, dumped, yet fell in love with. Not to mention the fake Boston/Keith who totally pulled the wool over her eyes, which luckily for her, she managed to find out about in the nick of time even if it was by pure accident. He was a total fraud.

It was at times like this she wished she had siblings, someone she could confide in. If what Boston had told her was true then there would be no doubt in this kind of situation, his entire family would be there for him. He was lucky and she was jealous.

Nevertheless, she was all alone and all her emotions were a jumbled mess.

"Aargh!" She yelled out to the empty room before pulling the covers back over her head to keep reality out.

Before she could drive herself too crazy, Liz called wanting to see how her weekend went.

"Actually do you and Claire have time for dinner tonight, have I got a story for you?" she said.

"Is it about Uncle Jack, because I love those ones."

"Come over and I'll tell you," she said.

"We'll be there, or at least I will," Liz said.

The doorbell rang and she felt so much better her friends were now here and with food.

"Okay, what's the big mystery?" Claire said. "Liz wouldn't tell me anything."

"Because I didn't know anything," Liz grumbled.

"Did the romantic weekend away go better than expected and now you're thinking of moving in together?" Claire said, excited.

"Tell me he didn't propose," Liz said, just as excited.

Alyssa would have laughed if she wasn't still so upset at being duped.

"It was neither, but I do have a story to tell you."

"Okay, hit us," Claire said, as they all got comfy.

"Well, let's just say that the truth is stranger than fiction," she said. "As you know, I recently found out there were two Bostons running around and after sorting out which was which, I gave the fake one the flick and went away with the real Boston."

"That's right," Liz said.

"I remember," Claire said.

"What does this have to do with your romantic weekend away?" Liz said, as both friends now felt a shiver of foreboding.

"I can't believe I'm about to say this, but you guys were right."

"Huh?" Claire said, confused.

"Our car broke down on the way to our romantic rendezvous and the woman who kindly stopped to help could only take Boston to the nearest town for help, so I was left with the car," she said.

"What?" Liz said.

"Why were you left behind?" Claire said.

"Her car was tiny and I couldn't fit," Alyssa said.

"Seriously?" Liz raised a sceptical eyebrow.

"It's true. And it probably would've been very uncomfortable even if I had gone with them," she said. "Anyway, while they were gone, I got bored and so I snooped and found his wallet that he accidentally left behind. Let's just say I found out I stupidly mixed up the Bostons like you said. The fake was the one I thought was real, whose real name is actually Keith Wong."

"Oh no," Liz gasped.

"What did you do? Are you okay?" Claire said, shocked.

"I was completely shocked. I found the fake business cards like the one he gave me in his wallet. Then I rummaged through his bag and what I found was even more disgusting," she said.

"What?"

"What did you find?"

Alyssa wanted to giggle at the look on her friends' faces, yet was still kicking herself at her own stupidity.

"He had a video camera with him and a lot of women having sex."

"That's disgusting," Liz said, screwing up her face.

"Definitely icky. What did you do?" Claire said.

"I deleted them all off, waited for him to return with the tow truck and as soon possible, rented a car and came home."

"What did Boston, I mean, Keith say?" Liz said.

"Yes, did he try to pretend it was all a misunderstanding?" Claire said.

"I didn't give him a chance. I was already on my way home *alone* when I talked to him, catching him out about his name before hanging up."

"Good for you," Liz nodded.

"What a sleaze," Claire said.

"Sleaze is the right word," she said. "Did I mention that when he returned with the tow truck that his clothes were all askew?"

Her friends gasped.

"Yes, he had a quickie with the good Samaritan."

"Oh Lys, I'm so sorry," Liz said, sympathetic.

"Yes, me too. No wonder you needed our company. Are you okay?" Claire said.

"Yes and no," she said, glum. "This whole thing and finding out that I was wrong about the wrong man is just so..."

She didn't have to say anything else. Her friends understood.

"What a jerk," Liz scowled.

"I know," Claire said. "I'm just relieved you didn't do something stupid like agree to be videoed."

"Yes, I have to say the grossest part is this guy was taping sex with all those women." Liz said.

All the women screwed up their faces at that.

"Do you think they knew?" Liz said.

"I don't know. I didn't watch it. Like I said, I scanned through it, saw what it was and then deleted it," she said.

"Good for you. Hopefully those women can now rest easy whether they knew they had been taped or not," Claire said. "Who knows what he does with it?"

"Makes you want to report him to the police," Liz said, angry.

"Anyway, back to the matter at hand," Claire said, trying to get the conversation back on track. "What are you going to do about the fake/real Boston?"

"That's what I don't know," Alyssa sighed. "I mean, I was so angry at him and dumped him. I can't see him wanting to patch things up, especially since I accused him of not being him."

"Oh honey," Liz sympathised.

"Don't worry, Lys. There's plenty more fish in the sea," Claire said, trying to be supportive and optimistic.

"That's the problem though?" she said, miserable. "I threw away the one I should have kept."

"But you didn't know," Liz said.

"I know, but it still doesn't make me feel any better."

The three friends spent the rest of the night cheering Alyssa up until she felt at least a little better.

Chapter Twenty-one

Once again the four Chan siblings were back together in London, only this time it was because of Indi and Jason's baby celebration. While the girls impatiently waited for their chance to interrogate Boston on Alyssa, the boys managed to run interference especially since Boston was staying with Phoenix in Boston's old place, which he kept as his London base. Now they were spending as much time together as possible and Boston couldn't be happier his brother was now living so much closer.

"By the way, Nix, how's your new job with Tony Santamaria working out?" Boston said. He had set up a job interview for his brother with a friend, but that was all. It had been up to Phoenix to sell himself and Tony to agree to hire him.

"Fantastic." The smile on Phoenix's face said it all.

"Not only is Tony an awesome mentor, but investment finance is totally my calling. Even Tony thinks so."

"I'm glad," he smiled. "Tony is a good man."

"He says that since I'm such a protégé I need to live it up while I can, before I become a superstar and don't have time for such luxuries," Phoenix laughed.

"There's the Nix confidence we all know and love," Boston chuckled.

"Sometimes I think it's a little weird that you found your niche now as more of an investor like me only you like to also sometimes buy and sell companies," Phoenix said. "Whereas I enjoy playing with other people's money."

"I know, me too. I never in a million years thought I'd enjoy investing in entrepreneurs, although in saying that, now that I've got a good handle on what to watch out for, I can tell you some of the people you really just have to stay completely away from, no matter what smoke they're trying to blow up your arse," he said.

"Really?" Phoenix said, his interest piqued.

"Yes. Some of my earlier investments which bombed like to keep coming back to me to try and get me to invest in their next pie in the sky idea and then they get really angry when I say no. They seem to think that since I did it once, even though they failed, I'd not only still back them as if I'm an unlimited money tree, but I also wouldn't question them on their failures or the notable holes in their business proposals," he sighed. "To be honest, I wouldn't be here or where I am today without Jason and Lucas. It was their belief in my gut feeling that started this. Without them, I probably would be working somewhere being a boring accountant or maybe a business analysis, which now that I'm not, I think I would have been bored out of my tree. This is definitely what I'm supposed to be doing."

"I hear you," Phoenix said. "I really thought I wanted to be an accountant, but being with Tony has really opened my eyes. Clearly I still love numbers and that type of thing, but what I'm doing right now is a lot more exciting especially since I'm playing with other people's money. I wouldn't even have thought to have done it if it weren't for you."

Seeing Phoenix try hard not to get too misty eyed in front of his brother, Boston pulled him in for a hug.

"Hey, pay it forward, right? Lucas and Jason helped me, so I'm helping you," Boston said. "So, what time's this celebration dinner?"

"Seven." Phoenix looked at his watch. "We'd better start getting ready. Have we got the present sorted?"

"What do you mean 'we'? I have," Boston said, using his big brother scolding and teasing tone.

"Exactly, 'we'," Phoenix chuckled.

The celebration was being held at a renown Chinese restaurant which the Kwong Lee family hired out for the night and Boston breathed a sigh of relief, thankful that the distraction of organising the dinner meant both his older sisters were too busy to hound him anytime soon about Alyssa. However, he was sternly warned as soon as they both greeted him.

"This looks great, Inds. I've been looking forward to a good Chinese meal," Boston said.

Although Indi was smiling and showing off Christopher, she was still looking at him, searching his face as only big sisters could do.

"You do realise that you're not looking too crash hot. Still missing Alyssa?"

He wanted to groan, but then Montana joined them.

"Yes, and don't think you're off the hook just because you're staying with Nix, either. You'll be giving us all the details tomorrow at lunch," Montana said.

"Oh dear, didn't I tell you I have a morning flight? Sorry," he said, feigning sadness.

"Liar. Jase has already told me that you're not leaving until first thing Monday morning," Indi said.

"What a big mouth," he scowled.

"Who's a big mouth?" Jason said, smiling and kissing his wife then taking the baby from her.

"You," Indi giggled.

"What did I do?" Jason said, nonplussed.

"Told Indi I'm not leaving until early Monday morning," Boston scowled.

"Oh that. Well, she caught me off guard," Jason grinned.

"What?" Indi huffed, feigning annoyance. "All I said was 'what time does Boston leave? We can have everyone over for lunch'."

"See, off guard," Jason chuckled. "I didn't know she was using her wily sister tricks."

"I'm surprised you didn't realise what she was up to since you're the baby in your family," Boston teased.

"I know you guys like to think that, but seriously, I don't think any family acts like yours. Ours is more *genteel*."

Jason's jibe earned him a nudge and a scowl from his wife.

"You're so lucky you're holding the baby," Indi said.

"And why do you think I am?" he teased. "I know you Chan siblings. It's best to have a shield where you can and now that we have the world's cutest baby, I intend to use him as a shield as often as possible."

Boston was amused Indi looked torn between love for her husband and scowling at him.

While they enjoyed catching up with Jason's friends and family, during dinner Boston and Phoenix stayed close to each other loving being together since they knew it was only for a short while.

The next day at lunch the interrogation was unable to be avoided and no matter how hard Boston tried to dance around and avoid his sisters' attempts, it was futile.

"Right, let's get down to it. How's it going with Alyssa?" Montana said.

"Yes, did you confess?" Indi said.

"Let's just say that before I could confess, she had already worked out that I wasn't me," he said, hedging.

"What does that mean?" Montana said, confused.

"It seems she remembered meeting 'me', only it wasn't 'me'."

"Okay, now I'm totally confused," Indi said. "I think you need to start at the beginning because last time we saw you, you were feeling guilty about not telling her the truth, that you weren't her boyfriend."

"Yes, and now you're saying there's two of you? What did you do? Clone yourself?" Montana said.

"Close," he said, relieved his brothers-in-law hadn't spilt the beans to his sisters about his last confession to them.

As expected, as soon as his sisters heard the latest update, they were ready to go and find Alyssa and not let her go until she had seen reason or at least knew that she was being conned by the wrong man. He wouldn't put it past Indi and Montana to also ensure that Alyssa knew without a doubt that she and Boston belonged together whether Alyssa agreed or not.

Although he wasn't too worried about his sisters' plans, there was still a concern that they would somehow manage to track Alyssa down and give her a stern talking to. Not only would that be embarrassing, but he was sure

Alyssa would never talk to him again.

One of the reasons Boston was leaving so early on Monday morning was to spend as much time as possible with Phoenix however, now his brother was going out after dinner.

"I knew it." Boston rolled his eyes. "You're ditching us."

"What? But I thought we were having a boys' night?" Lucas said, baffled.

"I can still do both because, let's face it, you're all old fuddy duddies, so this should all be wrapped up in an hour," Phoenix teased.

"I am not!" Jason huffed.

"Me either," Lucas said.

"But you are now *family* men," Phoenix said.

"True," Lucas said.

"Well, I'm not," Boston scowled.

"You might as well be, since you're moping over Alyssa so let's face it, you're basically one or two steps away from being *them*," Phoenix laughed, pointing at their brothers-in-law.

"Ouch Nix, that hurts," Boston said, trying hard not to smile.

"I like to think of us as *role models*. Men you can aspire to be," Lucas loftily said.

"Yes," Jason said. "We're the gold standard."

Now it was Phoenix's turn to snort as they all laughed.

"Just what exactly are you up to which trumps hanging

out with us?" Boston said, curious.

"Do you remember Scott Yang from high school? We played soccer together. Apparently he and a friend are in town, so I said I'd meet up with them."

"So you were always planning on ditching us?" Lucas said, raising his eyebrows.

"No, I told Scott I'd see what you guys wanted to do but I figured that you know, since you're all *old*, you probably wouldn't be up to a night out. You'd all probably want a cup of tea and then off to bed," Phoenix laughed.

"He's got a point," Jason shrugged.

"Let's face it, even thinking about clubbing has me exhausted right now," Boston said.

"You see, fuddy duddies," Phoenix smiled.

"You win. You go and live it up like the young thing you are," Lucas grinned. "I'm sure Jason has some video games we can play."

"Whoa, whoa, whoa, I didn't say I had to leave right now," Phoenix said, his competitive side showing and not wanting to miss out.

They all laughed and went to game.

While Boston flew home sad to leave his family and still miserable he had no Alyssa, his loving family were already discussing ways to meddle.

"We need to help him," Montana said. "And think of something soon."

"I agree," Indi said.

"But what?" Phoenix said. "None of us have ever met her. Maybe she's not 'the one'."

"Oh please," Montana snorted. "You've heard his story. Of course she's 'the one'. They had a moment."

"She doesn't even believe he is himself," Phoenix said.

"Then maybe we need to help her?" Indi said.

"How? You can't just rock on up to her and say Boston is Boston and the man she thinks is Boston, isn't. She'll think you're crazy," Jason said, earning him a glare from his wife.

"We'll prove it," Montana said.

"Again, how? Why would she believe you? You could be making it all up, trying to con her," he said.

"You're not being very helpful," Montana scowled.

"I'm being realistic," Jason said.

"I could do it. I'm his brother," Phoenix said.

"And once again, I argue, how would she know you're telling the truth?" Jason said.

"I agree with Jason," Lucas said, earning him a scowl from his wife. "What we need is someone who she'd believe. However, since none of us have met her, it can't be us and since we don't know anyone who she knows…"

"Unless we can discredit the other Boston so she figures it out herself," Phoenix said, happy with his idea.

"But how would we do that?" Montana said.

"No idea," he said, now glum. Meddling was playing

havoc with his emotions.

"What about her uncle?" Indi said.

"What about him?" Jason said.

"Well, he did give Boston's name and more importantly has met him so he'd definitely be able to confirm which Boston is the fake."

"But do you think he'll help us? What if he's changed his mind or refuses to?" Lucas said.

"Someone needs to go over there," Montana said.

"Who?" Indi said.

"It can't be Lucas or me," Montana said.

"And I've just had a baby and aren't ready to fly with one," Indi said.

"And I've not been in my job long enough to ask for time off," Phoenix said.

"I guess that just leaves me," Jason sighed. "But I really don't think I can help."

"Don't worry, we'll come up with not only a great reason for you to be there, but to also have to meet Alyssa," Montana said.

"How about we all sit on it for now," Lucas said, to Jason's relief that his brother-in-law had his back.

"What? But Bossy's lost hope. He needs our help *now*," Phoenix said.

"But we seriously have no ideas," Lucas said. "If we wait, something will come to us."

"Lucas is right. No point charging off to New York. We could make everything worse and ruin everything. No, we need a good plan," Jason said.

Chapter Twenty-two

The next day Uncle Jack rang at the same time she arrived home from work.

"Hey sunshine."

"Uncle Jack, what's up?" she chirped.

"Can you take a few days off work next week?"

"Why?"

"Because I have a surprise."

"It had better not be another fake boyfriend," she scolded.

"No, it'll be a husband," he chuckled.

"Not funny," she said.

"Yes it is. Oh, and pack everything you need because you'll be staying here."

"Uncle Jack, that's incest and I've told you, I'm not interested in coming to any of your orgies," she giggled.

"Not funny. There'll be *no* girls."

"Are you finally getting the house completely steril-ised and need me to make sure it's done properly?" she teased.

"Very funny. Although it's not a bad idea, maybe I should take this opportunity to give the house a good sterilising inside and out," he chuckled.

"Okay, that's just grossed me out."

"Seriously, bring everything you need." He didn't see the frown on Alyssa's face.

"Okay," she said.

All week she ran through every single scenario she could possibly think of as a reason for Uncle Jack to want her to stay with him. He said she should come on Sunday and it was all so cryptic and mysterious that she didn't know whether to be frightened or excited.

"Uncle Jack! I'm here! Where's my surprise?" she shouted to an eerily empty house.

He came out of his office to welcome her.

"Sunshine! You made it. It's been so long since I've seen you," he said, giving her a big bear hug.

"So where's my surprise?" she said, excitedly looking around.

"It comes tomorrow. Now you're sure you have every-thing?" he said.

"Yes. What's this all about?" She was buzzing with anticipation.

"You'll see tomorrow," he said.

Her sense of excitement deflated like a popped balloon.

That night she couldn't sleep, she was like a kid at Christmas and the next morning she dressed and bounced down to the kitchen with the energy and excitement of a five-year old.

"It's tomorrow, Uncle Jack. Where's my surprise?" she said, once again bubbling in anticipation as her uncle sat at the table with his breakfast in front of him reading the newspaper.

"Just be patient. Let's have some breakfast first," he said, enjoying her excitement.

"Can I get a hint, *please*."

"No."

"Just a teeny one?"

"No," he smiled.

"Well, do I look all right?"

"You look as beautiful as always," he smiled.

She had every right to feel happy, she was going to be blown away.

After they had finished breakfast and she had driven him mad, it was finally time.

"Sunshine, it's time," he said, suppressing a chuckle when he saw her hesitate for a brief moment. "Come outside onto the terrace."

She tentatively followed, constantly and suspiciously looking all around before going forward, practically jumping out of her skin in anticipation.

"Where is it?" she said. "I can't see anything."

"Oh, my mistake, it must be inside," Jack grinned.

Turning, she quickly strode inside and as soon as she saw her surprise, she stood there frozen, wide-eyed in shock. Unable to speak, move or even think.

Standing in the middle of the room was an elderly Chinese man. He looked so handsome and distinguished in his grey suit. His salt and pepper hair was greyer on the temples and he wore a kind and gentle smile.

Jack chuckled at Alyssa's stunned reaction.

"Well, aren't you going to say hello to your father?"

"H-hello," she said, shy at finally being in the presence of her father until something switched on in her head and she quickly closed the gap, tightly hugging him with tears flowing like a river. After what seemed like an eternity, she finally released him. "I-I don't understand. How, why are you here? I-I thought you couldn't leave Asia?"

There were so many questions flying around her head, it seemed impossible to not pepper him with them all at once.

It was Jack who explained as she sat and tightly held her father's hand.

"He's retiring."

"Can he do that?" she said, before Jack could finish his explanation.

"Yes and no," he said, uncertain. "You see, you can retire but that doesn't mean your enemies won't come after you. Lyssa, your father's here secretly hence the reason why you can't leave the house either."

"So he's leaving again?" she said, tears starting to fall once again.

"We're not sure yet. There's a few things to work out," Jack said.

"Okay, I'll take what I can get. I need my phone to take some photos." Jumping up and then running upstairs to get it while the two men whispered.

Alyssa was beyond ecstatic to finally meet her father. She was going to be grilling him non-stop until he answered all her questions.

It was heaven having time with her father. He had been patient with all her questions and posing for all her photos. They shared the same sense of humour and were constantly laughing. She even scolded him about Stan Wong.

"It was an honest and genuine mistake," Frankie chuckled. "My contact got mixed up and sent the old Stan Wong instead of the young one. Although after seeing the picture of both Stans you're probably better off with neither."

She told them what happened with her memory and Boston Chan, both of them.

"Do you love him?" Frankie said, in a quiet gentle voice.

"How can you love someone who lied to you? None of it was real," she said, miserable.

Frankie then explained how he met Katherine and fell

madly in love.

"When I met your mother, it was love at first sight. I had never seen such a beautiful woman in my life and her smile knocked me off my feet. She was such a loving and kind person. A beautiful soul and I could never quite believe she wanted to be with *me*, even when I told her in all honesty it wasn't going to be easy. I was a Triad and that life was dark and ugly and she was the beautiful fragile butterfly," he said, as Alyssa felt herself tearing up. "She was such a naive innocent woman and we had many ups and downs, but when we boiled it down, we loved each other. It was that love which was the reason I sent you both away. To be able to live your lives, free and happy. Choices staying with me could never give you. Yes, I had many mistresses, not because I was unfaithful in my heart, but because it was what people expected. I needed to act normal so people didn't suspect I never stopped loving Katherine otherwise your lives would have been in constant danger. Soon people had completely forgotten we had ever met."

"You see, Lys, your father couldn't just leave the Triad and play happy families with you and Katherine," Jack said. "They would have come after him, you or both."

"I'm not proud of the life I've lived, but I knew nothing other than the Triad world. If I had managed to leave, I probably would never have survived in a normal job," Frankie said.

"You didn't even try! You're a coward!" she said,

furious before sobbing and knowing deep down, he was probably right. The life she knew may not have happened at all.

He didn't ask her to forgive him. He just accepted this was his path and his love for his wife and daughter meant sacrificing a life with them.

"What I'm trying to tell you is that if you truly love someone, your heart knows. It doesn't worry about all the superficial stuff. You heart knew the real Boston Chan, but your head was the one deceiving you," Frankie said. "You have no idea how many times I wished I had just left with you and your mother. Wished everything was different, that I wasn't a Triad. Sometimes I even wished my enemies would just kill me and then it would be all over. It's a harder life to live knowing you can't be with the ones you love the most. Even Jack's visits were bitter-sweet. As much as I longed to hear news about you and your mother, every time it left me with such melancholy, knowing I couldn't share any of that with you. Couldn't be the one to help with any problems or share in your joy."

Alyssa could see the pain and regret on his face.

"When your mother got sick, it was one of my worst fears, losing her. Even though we hadn't been together for years. It was why I left Asia for the first time, because I needed to see my one and only true love and it was my selfishness, which could have cost everyone I loved dearly."

Tears were streaming down Alyssa's face seeing the

sadness and heavy burden her father carried for all the choices made. Finally she understood the cost to them all and she too, wished it could have all been different.

Her father was right. Her heart had always known which Boston was the real one, but she had been letting her head mislead her because how was it possible to fall in love with not only a complete stranger, but one she couldn't remember.

That night Jack and Frankie were discussing Alyssa and Boston.

"This is all my fault," Frank sighed, sadness in his voice that he was the one sabotaging his daughter's happiness.

"How?" Jack said, even though he knew what his brother would say.

"Because of who I am. None of this would be happening if —"

"No. Don't do that. We can't change the past and even if we could, who's to say that you would have ever met Katherine."

"I miss her every day," he said, sad.

"I know."

"That's why we need to find a way for Alyssa to be with the man she loves," he said. "Are you sure that he's a good man?"

While Frankie may never have been really present in

his daughter's life, it didn't mean he didn't love her enough to want only the best for her.

"Yes," Jack said, with a firm nod. "Obviously it would have been easier if he wasn't so well-known or connected. Then your lifestyle wouldn't be such an issue, as such." He hoped he was lessening Frankie's guilt even a little.

"Well, that's not what it is," he sighed.

"No."

"I want to talk to this Boston Chan."

"What? No," Jack gasped. "You know you're supposed to be invisible."

"Yes, but if we met him, perhaps we can get his measure and find out once and for all if he really is good enough for Alyssa or would the horror of finding out her father is the head of a Triad put him right off her for good."

"That's true," Jack said, thoughtful. "But what if he blabs that he met you. You know, you as in the 'boss' not as Lys' father?"

"I'm willing to take the risk for Lyssa," Frankie said.

"Are you willing to possibly risk Lys' life?"

"For her future and a chance at love? Yes."

Chapter Twenty-three

Boston wasn't concentrating very well and decided fresh air was required. Upon his return from his walk and as he approached the building entrance, the door of a limousine opened and Jack Lee stepped out.

"If you have a moment, I'd like to talk to you in private," he said.

The situation made Boston uneasy, yet he agreed and got into the back of the limousine.

To his surprise, there was another older man in the car.

"Hello Jack, what's all this about?" Boston said, trying to hide his nervousness.

"We want to know what your intentions are towards Alyssa?" Jack said, getting straight to the point.

"I'm sorry?" It took him a moment to comprehend what Jack was actually saying to him.

"Your intentions."

"I have none at this point in time. Actually, it's died a natural death." He didn't add it was because she accused him of being a fake and dumped him.

The other man snorted and started rattling off what Boston could only assume was him being scolded.

Jack said something back before turning to Boston to speak again.

"You know, I picked you as the best man for Lys and at the first hurdle you give up? You don't deserve her."

Boston didn't need to sit here and be insulted.

"Okay, I really don't have to listen to this and it's not really any of your business."

"Do you love her?" the other man said, in a grouchy tone.

"I don't know who you are or what it has to do with you, but yes, I do," he said, with a heavy sigh.

"This is Lyssa's father, Frankie Lee," Jack said.

"Her father?" he said, astonished. "But she said she couldn't remember her father."

"Well, she finally did," Jack said. "Although we'd appreciate it if you didn't tell anyone that you've met him."

"Huh?" he said, confused.

"It's a long story and perhaps Lys will tell you about it sometime," Jack said. "Now back to Lys, why are you being so stupid?"

"*Excuse me?* I'm not being stupid. It's not like she's contacting me. Besides, she thinks I'm not even me."

Jack heaved a sigh at his niece's stubbornness.

Boston could see Jack cursing to himself over the situation and realised that the older man knew about the 'mix-up'.

"So you know we had an argument over 'me' and I haven't seen her since. I tried to contact her, but she wasn't home. And, before you get back on your high horse, don't blame me. *She's* the one who broke it off."

"That's because she's a Lee and they're renowned for their stubbornness," Jack said, now no longer angry at Boston.

Frankie rapidly spoke and Boston knew he wanted to know what was going on. Jack replied, looking just as annoyed, and then it seemed an agreement was made between them.

"You're right," Jack said, after finally finishing the conversation with his brother. "My brother wants me to tell you the truth so that you can understand before you make your final decision."

"Okay," he nodded.

"The reason you can't tell anyone about Frankie being here and the cloak and dagger secrecy is for all our safety. You see, Frankie is actually the head of a Triad."

"What?" Boston's mind exploded in shock. "Does Lys know?"

"Yes, although it was only after her mother's death that she was told and she's also only just met her father for the first time a few days ago as well."

"I don't understand," Boston said, bewildered.

As Jack explained the relationship between Katherine and Frankie and why Alyssa had never met her father after they left to live in America, Boston was trying hard to comprehend the situation.

"But that still doesn't help the fact that her father is, you know," he said.

Jack spoke to Frankie who rapidly spoke back and Boston could only assume Frankie was telling Jack to do something.

"What I'm about to tell you, you're not allowed to repeat," Jack said.

Honestly, the way the whole conversation was going, Boston wasn't sure if he even wanted to know.

"Ah, I'm not sure —"

"This could be the answer to your problems so you and Lyssa can be together," Jack said.

Hope flared through Boston and he badly wanted to grab and hold onto it.

"This trip and seeing Lys, Frankie has decided he wants to retire," Jack said.

Once again shock rumbled through Boston.

"Can you do that?" he whispered. Was this unlike the movies that made it seem an impossibility? "But it still doesn't change the fact that if it comes out that you do business or associate with Triads and Frankie is the head of one of those gangs, then me and my families' reputations will be tarnished."

"Well, we don't quite have all the details worked out but essentially, I can deny I ever knew I was doing business with someone who isn't just a simple businessman and Frankie, well, he's planning to die."

"What!" Boston said, shocked. "Lys will be devastated."

"Not for real," Jack chuckled, pleased to see that Boston was thinking of his niece and not himself. "He'll fake his own death so no one will know he's alive and can start over. The plan is to smuggle him out of Asia to America, but like I said, the details need to be worked out. That's why you can't say anything. If you do, you put everyone including yourself in danger." He was laying it on very thick, but he didn't want Boston blabbing even accidentally because people may come after him to get to Alyssa.

"Does Lys know?"

"No. We don't want to get her hopes up. Now if we can pull this off, are you willing to have a relationship with her?"

Once again, hope flared inside Boston, but this time it was more like fireworks exploding.

"There's still a few things we need to sort out, like the fact she doesn't believe I'm me," he said.

"Although I shouldn't be telling you this because it's something you two need to sort out, she recently discovered she'd made a mistake in thinking you were a fake and the other guy was the genuine article."

"Is she okay?" He couldn't even be happy at the news because now he was worried about her. "How…" He stopped himself asking a million probably unanswerable questions. "I think I need time to think and when you come up with your solution let me know. Like you, I don't think it's right to give Lys false hope." Or me, he wanted to say, but didn't.

"Agreed. I'll be in touch," Jack said.

It warmed Jack's heart that Boston truly did seem to be putting Lyssa's feelings first. Now that was the kind of man he wanted for his niece.

After his meeting with Jack and Frankie, Boston's mind was full of hope and confusion. It was unbelievable what he had learned and knew this was one of those things he had to share with his family. This was too big a situation for him to deal with alone. He was having trouble processing it all.

Heading back to London, he kept second-guessing himself as to whether he was doing the right thing or not. Jack had wanted to keep this a secret and although Boston understood, he also knew he needed to get his brothers-in-law advice and Phoenix would also be able to keep a secret.

Letting Phoenix know he was on his way and to get Jason and Lucas involved as discreetly as possible, his brother made the arrangements.

"Okay, what's with all the cloak and dagger?" Phoenix said, once everyone had gathered and Lucas had dialled in from Italy.

"What's the update?" Lucas said, concerned.

"What I'm about to tell you can seriously go no further than us. You have to swear not to tell the states, otherwise I can't tell you."

Boston's tone showed just how important this was and so everyone agreed.

"We promise," Phoenix said.

"So I recently had a visit from Alyssa's uncle and her father…"

"And?" Phoenix said, as everyone was eager to hear more.

"This is the part where it gets complicated and why you can't tell anyone. I'm not even supposed to be telling you, but I figured you have the right to know because it could affect your families and businesses," he said.

Jason and Lucas instantly recognised the gravity of the situation.

"Go ahead, Bos, lay it on us," Jason said.

"They told me the truth about Alyssa and her father, Frankie. How she left when she was too young to really remember him and hadn't ever met him until now. What she learnt after her mother's death was the reason why. It turns out that Frankie is the head of a Triad gang. Which one, I don't know and don't care," he said.

"Wow," Phoenix said, shocked.

"The fact that he is who he is and if anyone gets wind of it or our association with him because of Alyssa, means that our reputations could be damaged for good."

"Oh Bos," Jason sympathised. "You know that's not true. Sure it'll be damaging, but if someone like Kai can manage to overcome his past with Donnie, so can we. I'm not saying it's easy, but it can be done."

"No." He shook his head. "You guys know it'll be damaging not only for your businesses, but families. I don't want to be the one to bring everyone down just because of Alyssa's father."

"What did you tell them?" Lucas said.

"There wasn't much I could say, I was so shocked by the news. Jack told me that Frankie wants to retire," he said.

"Can you do that?" Jason said.

"He said that they hadn't quite worked out the logistics, but it in effect it may have to include faking his own death."

"Wow," Phoenix said.

"They did ask if they managed to pull it off, could I see myself being with Lys," he said, wanting them all to know the truth.

"What did you say?" Lucas said.

"That it all depended on their plans and decisions. I wasn't about to give myself or Lys false hope that we could ride off into the sunset together. This whole thing could be just too big a hurdle to overcome," he said. "Like

I said, this whole thing doesn't just affect me, it affects both the Kwong Lee and Romero families."

"Oh Bos, I'm sorry you have got such a difficult decision to make," Phoenix said.

"Yes, and I have to say, your story is a heck of a lot more complicated than ours ever were," Jason said.

"But we have your back, Bos. Always," Lucas said.

Boston felt himself getting misty eyed over the love and support he was getting, which made him even more determined to protect their families.

A month later Lucas and Phoenix were together in Lucas' hotel suite discussing Boston while Montana and Indi had gone shopping.

"He's still miserable," Phoenix said, hurting for his brother.

"I know. I just wish there was something we could do for him," Lucas sighed, but this wasn't just a simple case of locking two people in a room until they saw the light and realised they loved each other. This was a case of things being out of everyone's control which was why everyone felt helpless, none more so than Boston.

"Where's Jase?" Phoenix said, looking around and realising that his brother-in-law wasn't here yet.

"Indi said something urgent came up," Lucas said, as Phoenix frowned.

"I hope everything's all right."

"Me too."

A knock at Lucas' hotel room door sounded.

"That'll be Jase," he said, getting up to answer it.

"Sorry, I'm late. Kai called me and then we got cut off. I've been trying to reach him, but he's not answering," Jason said, worry etched on his face.

After years of rivalry, Jason and Kai were now not only close, but also loosely related since Kai was Jason's cousins' half-brother.

"Is he in trouble?" Lucas said, now just as worried for Kai.

"Should we call the authorities?" Phoenix said.

Jason's cell phone rang and he quickly answered it.

"Kai? Are you okay?"

"I'm fine, just had a bit of a scary and mysterious meeting, that's all," Kai said, to Jason's relief. "Listen, are you alone?"

"No, I'm with Lucas and Phoenix. Why?"

"Phoenix? That's Indi's younger brother, right? Doesn't she also have another one, Boston?" Kai said.

"Yes, now what's going on?" Jason was back to being worried again.

"I need to talk to you *privately*," Kai said.

"If this is something we can all help you with, I don't mind if they listen in as long as you don't," Jason said.

"I not sure if you really want them to know —"

"I'm putting you on speaker. Kai, what's going on?" Jason said, torn between worried and annoyed.

"Kai, it's Lucas, are you okay? Do you need help?" he said, now worried that perhaps he was in trouble.

"Hi guys. I'm okay, not in any trouble, well, no more than normal," he chuckled, but the silence ensured he realised that everyone was being serious.

"Just get to the point," Jason said.

"Okay, so as you know I don't really associate with certain people anymore since I became one of the family," Kai said. "And so let's just say that it was a bit of a fright when in the middle of talking to you I met an important underworld figure, shall we say. That's why I had to go."

"Are you okay? Are you in some kind of trouble?" Jason's anxiety had now ramped up.

"Like I said, I'm fine and to repeat, no I'm not in any trouble but my knees were shaking, not that I'd admit it," Kai chuckled. "But it's good to know you still care if something should happen to me."

The teasing didn't relax Jason at all.

"What did he want?" Phoenix said, asking the question they all wanted to know the answer to.

"It's actually quite confusing and I'm not even sure why he came to me," Kai said, puzzled.

"What did he want?" Jason said, his worry quickly ramping up again.

"It seems this person has asked for me help in trying to get someone out of Asia in the most invisible manner."

"Why you?" Lucas said, perplexed.

"That's what I said, and his answer was that no one would think twice about me helping him."

"Why would you want to? Who is this person? Are you being blackmailed?" Jason said, various scenarios sprinting through his head about why Kai had been chosen. Before Kai became a Kwong Lee, he hadn't lived an honest life. Had his past now come back to bite him on the arse?

"He didn't make much sense. Just that this person needed to disappear where no one would find them. He mentioned possibly America," Kai said.

"Oh my God," Lucas said, stunned as the pieces came together in his mind. "Was your meeting with *Frankie Lee*, the you know who?" He whispered the latter part as everyone looked wide-eyed in understanding.

"Yes, how did you know?" Kai said, shocked. Was the man psychic?

Lucas exchanged looks with his brothers-in-law, they were now all on the same page and understood what this meant.

"Actually, I think we can solve this whole mystery for you and I know you can keep it a secret," Jason said, as Lucas nodded. "You see, Indi's brother, Boston recently met the woman who we all think is his *one*."

That made Kai chuckle.

"Anyway, we've only just found out recently that she's Frankie's daughter —"

"What!" The shock in Kai's voice wasn't surprising.

"It's a long story," Jason sighed. "Another reason you have to keep it a secret because no one knows he had a daughter or at least, as far as we can tell, remembers."

"He sent them away years ago to keep them safe. She's also only just re-met her father for the first time recently," Lucas said.

"What does that have to do this situation?" Kai said.

"Well as much as we all think that Boston and Alyssa belong together, if her parentage came out then it could damage all our families' reputation by association or even worse, Alyssa could be a target for any of Frankie's enemies," Jason said.

"So Boston knows Frankie is her father and who he is?" Kai said, surprised.

"He's only just found out at the same time Alyssa re-met her father. It's a really long story. The crux of the matter is basically, I think Frankie wants to disappear so that Bos and Lys can be together," Lucas said.

"But won't that just make it worse? Someone is bound to recognise Frankie. I mean, yes, he's known in Asia but you know, people travel, they might see him on the street or in the background of some random social media thing and recognise him, even if it's years later," Kai said, concerned.

"You make it sound like a movie," Phoenix said.

"Well, you hear stories all the time that people are found even after decades on the run. Usually by complete accident," Kai said.

"He's got a point," Lucas said.

"What did you say to Frankie?" Jason said, wanting to get back to Kai's meeting.

"I said, I didn't think I could help him, that I don't roll like that anymore," Kai said, now feeling guilty.

"Was he upset?" Jason said.

"No. Well, he looked sad and resigned to the fact."

"Maybe we need to talk to Frankie's brother, Jack," Jason said.

"Whoa. Do you mean *Jack Lee*? *He's* Frankie's *brother*?" It seemed the bombshells were dropping all around Kai right now.

"Yes," Jason said.

"Wow. I never even suspected," Kai said, astonished.

Now the other men were shocked Kai knew who Jack was and so he explained how he knew him.

"From what we understand, no one is meant to know," Jason said.

"And now everyone seems to know," Lucas muttered.

"What about Boston?" Phoenix said, worried that they were leaving his brother in the dark.

"It would be better if he didn't know until we have something concrete for him. The less people know, the better," Jason said, then looked hard at Phoenix. "Promise you won't tell him, Nix."

"I won't," Phoenix said. "I want my brother to be happy."

"We all do, Nix. But we also need a plan and patience,

which I know is hard for you," Lucas said, clapping him on the shoulder.

"Okay, here's what we'll do," Jason said. "We'll try and make contact with Jack to see what he knows and if we can clarify the situation a bit more. Kai, you just keep up your end of going about your business. Don't seek him out, but should you *happen* to run into Frankie again, you may want to subtly let him know in some way that you now understand the situation a little more and may be available in some *limited* capacity."

"Got it," Kai said.

"Everyone has to keep this under their hat. No telling wives or sisters," Jason said, stern.

After Kai had disconnected the three men looked at each other in silence.

"Well, you have to admit, this is one heck of a Chan sibling love story," Lucas said.

"A lot messier than mine," Jason said, relieved he wasn't Boston.

"I'm never going to be this complicated," Phoenix said, shaking his head.

"It's not like you aim for this kind of situation, Nix," Lucas chuckled.

"Yes. You're a Chan, so you'll just find yourself in it whether you like it or not," Jason laughed.

"Right, so back to the task at hand. Who wants to talk to Jack?" Lucas said, as he and Phoenix looked at Jason.

"I guess that'll be me," he sighed.

"Well, I'd do it, but unless he comes to Italy it'll be easier for you," Lucas said. "Plus if we need Kai then it's best you're the point of contact."

"Let's just hope we can pull this off," Jason said.

Chapter Twenty-four

Having time out from her life and getting to know her father better was exactly what Alyssa needed. It seemed that her parents' love story even though she still didn't quite agree with it, made her realise that love, the real kind, was give and take, compromise or even worse, sacrifice.

The nights were the worst because all she could think about was Boston, and how much compromise or even sacrifice he had made to his life for her. A stranger. It didn't matter that it was only for a week. He had still altered his routine for her. In return she had doubted his sincerity and integrity and given him the old heave-ho like a bag of rubbish being taken out, which made her feel guilty every time she thought about it.

While she may now better understand the complex-ities which kept her own parents apart, she also realised she didn't have those same excuses. There was no reason for not being able to at least apologise to Boston for her horrible accusations and the way she had treated him. The only thing stopping her was her fear that he would turn around and treat her with the same disdain she had him.

Still didn't he deserve to know she now knew the 'real' truth? Shouldn't she do the right thing and at least apologise? He had been doing something completely selfless for a complete stranger, only to have her accuse him of treachery. Round and round her thoughts went with no definite answer. Perhaps she should just let sleeping dogs lie and yet, she knew it was just her cowardice talking.

Heaving a sigh which sounded like the weight of the world was on her shoulders, she closed her eyes hoping some sort of answer would come to her in her sleep. It was the same hope every night since she'd found out the truth and yet, knew she would wake again with no answer.

After yet another night of restless sleep, Alyssa finally had to admit that deep down she just wanted an excuse to be able to see and talk to Boston again. Her subconscious and body knew that he was the one for her. No one had ever made her feel so cherished.

Deciding she was going to search him on the Internet, wondering why she hadn't thought to do this when she first realised there were two Bostons? It may have saved her a whole lot of time and heartache. She was stunned by the results that turned up. Seeing all the images of him just made her heart beat faster and wish once again, she hadn't cut him out of her life. There were articles on him from respected outlets and so she read them only to find that he was not only successful, but according to the reporters, also related to some very wealthy families.

Remembering how close he was to his siblings, Alyssa couldn't help but wonder if he had told them about her. If she ever met them, would they slam the door in her face because of the way she treated him? She had always wanted siblings and Boston being so close to his was a bonus.

Her biggest problem was how was she going to approach him and apologise for her stupidity? Sighing and knowing she still had no ideas, she could only mope and wallow.

After visiting Boston, Jack and Frankie had a long and hard discussion about the future and how to make it work for Alyssa. They both agreed that Alyssa and Boston belonged together, but it was Frankie's life that was the stumbling block. It was possible that no one would ever link father and daughter as no one had yet. However, they both knew it would be better to try and avoid that accidental connection in any way possible, but how? Another problem would be, if another route was chosen, would this then end up bringing the link to the world.

The choices and decisions were more than difficult

and both brothers had pros and cons about any ideas they had. The only thing they both knew was that Frankie needed to retire. Being who he was and what he had done in his life, even retiring wouldn't make him less of a target. People wanted payback and thinking he was now an old man and not as powerful as he once was, who had an army of loyal soldiers protecting him, meant he now had weaknesses to be exploited. This led to the only con-clusion both brothers had. Frankie had to die, or at least, fake his own death.

They were going to also need help getting him out of Asia and to New York.

It was Frankie's suggestion that he approach Kai Kwong Lee to test the waters. The man used to be known as Kai Chen, Donnie Chen's son until it was revealed that he was in fact related to the Kwong Lee family through Jimmy's brother-in-law, Tony Wang. With the Kwong Lee family's blessing, Kai changed his surname to theirs even though technically he wasn't a Kwong Lee, but Kai didn't want to be a Chen any more than he did a Wang. Frankie felt Kai could be trusted more than another person, but as both brothers knew, anyone could have loose lips for the right price or incentive.

No matter what the choice, this whole situation needed to be set up with patience. However, seeing Alyssa so miserable not only from having no Boston and her father returning back to Asia, Jack decided he was going to take her to London for a break. What he didn't tell her was that he was also going to get in touch with Jason Kwong Lee and hopefully subtly see which way the wind blew in regards to his possible help.

Although Alyssa was grateful to Uncle Jack for this long weekend in London to try and take her mind of her father's departure, she really couldn't seem to muster up the right amount of genuine enthusiasm for the trip.

"You don't need to take me away, Uncle Jack. I'm fine right here," she said.

"No, a change of scenery would do you good. You've been moping ever since your father left and I know it's not just because of that. If it was, I would leave you alone. No, this is also because of Boston," he said.

Even hearing his name aloud made her heart ache for what could have been.

"Fine," she sighed. "But you'll be regretting it when I charge up tens of thousands of pounds on designer clothes."

"I don't care. Buy whatever you want. Anything to see you smile again, sunshine."

His answer did make her smile, knowing he truly would spend every penny he owned to cheer her up.

"Thanks, Uncle Jack. I guess this trip won't be so bad," she said.

"That's my girl."

Alyssa actually found herself excited to be in not only another country, but on a shopping holiday once they landed and checked in at Claridges. Maybe Uncle Jack was right and all she needed was a change of scenery to get out of the funk she was in. He told her he had some business to attend while here and so he'd meet her for dinner.

"Not a problem," she smiled. "There's a ton of stores calling my name."

"See, there's that smile I've been missing. Does your uncle know you or what?"

"You were right. This is just what I needed."

"Great. I'll call you later this afternoon to check on you," he said, giving her a quick kiss and hug.

"Hey, aren't your forgetting something," she grinned.

"What?"

"Your card," she giggled, holding out her hand.

"You can use your own card and I'll pay it off like I always do," he sighed, pulling out his wallet. "You don't need mine."

"I believe you said I could buy tens of thousands of dollars of clothing and we both know my limit is nowhere near what yours is."

"If you can max this out, I'll be comatose. Lose it and I'll kill you. Remember, I know people," he winked.

"So do I," she laughed. "Thanks Uncle Jack. Have a good day and I hope your business goes well."

"It better, since I'm now going to be in debt for who knows how much thanks to your shopping. Can you at least try to buy on sale?"

"Sure. That means that I can buy even more." She laughed at his look of resignation. "I'll see you at dinner."

"It's going to be takeout if you spend too much."

"Takeout it is. Love you, Uncle Jack."

"Love you too, Lys."

Jason was surprised to find he had a meeting with Jack Lee and wondered if he should pretend he didn't know who he was since they had never done business together before.

"Jase, what's up?" Lucas said, answering his phone.

"My diary shows I have a meeting with Jack Lee and since we've never done business together, I'm wondering if this is personal or not? What do you think?" he said, needing Lucas' thoughts.

"That's a hard one and a very big coincidence. Are you sure it's Alyssa's uncle and not someone else with the same name? If it is, you may just have to play it by ear. If it is personal, then I'm guessing he's going to suss you out," Lucas said.

"But according to Boston, he wasn't supposed to tell us about Frankie, which means I'm not supposed to know," he said.

"True. Maybe he wants to see if Boston did blab?"

"Maybe," Jason sighed.

"Let me know how it goes and then perhaps we may have a better handle on what's going on."

"Okay. Thanks Lucas."

"Ciao."

After his meeting with Jack Lee, Jason sat there still comprehending what was discussed. He had never had a meeting like the one he just had and decided to call Lucas to let him know what had happened.

Lucas and Jason had made a pact years ago that if they talked to each other as confidants then their secrets would be safe with the other. No sharing with wives or anyone else. It was only because every now and then they needed to vent or confide something and they both knew how close their wives and siblings were. It was at times like this he was grateful for his close bond with his brother-in-law.

"How did it go?" Lucas said.

"It really was a poorly disguised attempt at a business meeting like you predicted," he said. "In the beginning it was all niceties dancing around Jack's real reason for coming. He was trying to subtly work out if I was open to helping them. In the end I had to say, 'Look, let's stop dancing around and put all our cards on the table'. Honestly the strain of tiptoeing around the elephant in the room was tiring."

"Good on you. Then what happened?"

Jason explained the rest of the meeting.

"I have no idea what you mean," Jack said, his poker face was good, but his eyes flickered with nervousness.

"Boston's told me about you and your brother."

Anger rose swiftly as Jack scowled.

"So much for being able to trust him with a secret. You do realise that the more people who know, the more chance this gets out and puts everyone in danger."

The threat didn't faze Jason at all. In fact, it made him angry.

"Oh no, you don't. You don't get to blame him. He was right to tell me especially since the safety and reputations of our families are involved. Not to mention that you both want *our* help and therefore we had a right to not only know, but be warned. And yes, I know that your brother has been in contact with Kai," Jason said.

Now it was Jack's turn to be surprised.

"Kai told you?" Did no one in this family know how to keep their lips zipped. He was shocked that no one had tried to kill Frankie by now.

"Of course, he did. And I wasn't about to let Kai walk into some kind of trap, if that's what it was. But since we now know the truth, it's now easier to discuss. What's your plan?" he said.

Hours later both men seemed satisfied about what they had agreed between them and the end solution wasn't quite what Jack thought would happen, but after much discussion both men realised that would probably be the best way forward so everyone wins. Now they just had to get all the pieces together and the players in the right position. Provided there were no leaks, they had time on their side.

"Well done, Jase. I would have said the same things you did. As you and Boston have said, this could affect us all, but the fact they also want Kai's help means it's a lot more dangerous for him," Lucas said.

"I agree and won't let either of them use Kai as a pawn. What I can't understand is that if Frankie had managed to slip out of the country this last time with no one knowing, why can't he do it again and just disappear?" he said.

"I see what you mean. Maybe they need the big show of him dying so no one would think twice?"

"Maybe. But we're not going to move too quickly on this because it might unknowingly bring attention to them or Kai. On the other hand, we can't be too slow either in case someone blabs or we get found out. Man, this is so stressful and all we've done is talk," Jason said.

"I know, but that's because this is all for Boston and Alyssa. I bet if we really didn't have any personal involvement we wouldn't be this worried."

"I know I'm not going to be sleeping well until I know this is all over and Kai is okay," he said.

"We all won't be. Hey, at least you have a good excuse for your sleepless nights, a newborn baby," Lucas said.

"True. What about you?" Jason knew that Lucas would also be worrying about him and Kai, which just showed how close they had become because of their wives. They truly felt like brothers.

"Oh, I'll just do what I always do, make sure my nights are filled with *distraction*," Lucas chuckled.

"I don't need to know," Jason laughed. "Thanks Luc."

"Anytime. That's what family is for. Ciao."

Jason sat in his chair and hoped that after all this, Boston and Alyssa could have their happily ever after.

Alyssa had been shopping all morning when she decided it was not only time for a break but she needed some sustenance. She hadn't had a huge shopping blowout in a long time and had forgotten how exhausting it could be, especially trying on all the clothes that she liked.

"Put that down" the woman at the table next to Alyssa scolded her friend.

"What?" the friend feigned innocence, making Alyssa smile.

"I know what you're doing?" the woman giggled. "Stop it."

"You don't know what I was doing," the friend grinned.

"You were sending your sister pics to see if she can buy the clothes cheaper in Italy."

"Fine, you caught me," the friend huffed, grinning.

"You know Jase can afford to buy you anything. Full retail price."

"True, but you of all people know you want any kind of discount you can get. And, these are *Italian* designers. It's not like I'm asking her to compare prices on everything I've got my eye on. Besides, Mon does it to me all the time. This is what we do. Sometimes we get a bargain and then we have to exchange purchases. It a great way to make sure we catch up with each other."

"You guys are the funniest family I know," the woman laughed. "How's your brother doing?"

"Miserable," the friend sighed. "Honestly, no one can think of a thing to get him out of this funk. What makes it worse is that we can't hate the woman because not only is it not her fault, but she's his *one*."

"I love how you guys call it that. It makes me laugh every time."

"I know, but it's true. We've all had lightning hit us. Jase keeps telling me that Bos' funk will magically disappear as soon as they make up," the friend giggled.

"I remember Jase's funk. Mum and dad were worried about him. Good thing for meddling families, right?" the woman teased.

Alyssa sat there smiling to herself at the conversation she couldn't help but overhear. What it must be like to not only have a sibling, but also be so close to them that they'd meddle in your life looking out for you.

"We want that for Bos. Unfortunately, the woman didn't recognise Bos' gesture as loving or even a gesture to her, which is understandable since she had amnesia. Personally, I think if she really his one, then she needs to reciprocate."

"But if she doesn't know that's what it was…"

"I know," the friend sighed again, then perked up slightly changing the topic. "The funniest thing about this whole thing is watching Nix seeing his brother so miserable and him saying that's not going to happen to him. We all can't wait until it's his turn and then we're going to make him eat all those confident words of his."

A phone sounded.

"Oh, we'd better get going. Mum's asking how far away we are. That's code for 'save me'," the woman laughed. "The kids have clearly run her ragged."

"Okay, let's go."

After the women had departed, Alyssa sat there knowing it had been rude to eavesdrop, but she enjoyed listening to the warm familiarity in the way the two women spoke.

The woman's brother sounded like he really could use cheering up if he was that miserable. What it must be like to have siblings who cared? What was even more astounding to Alyssa was the fact that the woman wasn't mad at whoever made her brother miserable. She was understanding, which to Lys seemed unfathomable. Most people wouldn't care about the girlfriend's feelings and to have her considered his *one*, what was that about? What if this woman was actually a terrible person and had pulled the wool over the brother's eyes? Wouldn't it be horrible if they got back together just because everyone else in the family thought she was his *one*.

Maybe that's what Alyssa needed to do to apologise. Make her own gesture. If nothing else, it could help get rid of some of the guilt she felt over her treatment of

Boston. Only what could she do? She'd talk to Uncle Jack and see what he thought, perhaps he could even come up with idea. No, she was better off talking to her friends, she shuddered to think of what Uncle Jack would come up with.

At dinner, Alyssa decided she couldn't wait to ask her friends for advice and therefore asked Uncle Jack instead and prayed he'd have something that wasn't icky and a good idea.

"Uncle Jack what would you do if someone had done a lovely thing for you, but you didn't realise it for what it was at the time? How would you do something nice for them in return?"

"It depends on what it was and who the person was? Can I be hopeful that we're talking about Boston Chan?" he said.

"Am I that transparent?" she sighed.

"Only to me, sunshine," he smiled. "Want to tell me what this is all about?"

"You see, I realise that he helped me after my accident even though he didn't have to. He put his life on hold for a week for a stranger," she said.

"Because he loves you."

She squashed down any hope that his words were truthful. Instead she huffed a little snort of disbelief.

"You can't fall in love with a stranger *and* in a week."

"Lys, we went over this with your father. Of course you can. I may not have done it, but you could say I fall in love *every* week or at least in *lust*," he grinned.

"Well, that's true," she giggled.

"And didn't you say that you fell in love with him?"

"Yes," she sighed.

"So what's the problem?"

"I think I need to make a gesture to apologise for dumping him and accusing him of not being him. And, if I love him, shouldn't I have ideas coming out the wazoo? And yet, I have zero, none, nada, zilch," she said, miserable.

"Let me think on it and perhaps tomorrow you'll get your answer."

"Okay."

Chapter Twenty-five

Boston was coming out of a shop when his phone started ringing, looking down to see it was Jason calling, he smiled and answered.

"Jase."

"Bos, I'm —"

Suddenly Boston yelled out in pain, now on the ground.

"Bos! Are you okay?" Jason said, yelling through the phone in a panic.

Boston found his phone, which he dropped and saw his screen was cracked in places.

"I'm fine, just embarrassed. I wasn't watching where I was going and tripped over, rolling my ankle pretty badly." He wanted to groan at his own idiocy, but was in too much pain.

"Do you want me to call someone?" Jason said.

"No, I'll call a cab and go to the hospital and get it checked out," he said.

"Okay, well keep me posted."

"Will do."

At the hospital embarrassed by his accident especially since it was his own fault, the doctor bandaged his ankle saying thankfully it was only a very bad sprain and he needed to keep his weight off it. Therefore he would need a few days rest at the very least.

The nurse arranged for him to have crutches and he was allowed to wait in the room and keep his foot raised until they organised his discharge papers.

He lay back on the bed wondering how he was going to manage with crutches over the next few days. Once he had arrived at the hospital, he called Jason while he waited for the doctor to reassure his brother-in-law that he was fine, but feeling like a complete idiot for something so stupid. Boston had to smile at firmly telling Jason to ensure that none of the family came over just to see him. Although at times like this he wished he still lived with Jason and Indi or was at least in the same city as one of his siblings knowing that they would have already arrived at the hospital before the doctor had even seen him. That was the blessing of being so close to his siblings.

Feeling peckish, he decided to go and get a snack from the vending machine.

Alyssa was at work thinking about what to have for lunch when the call came.

"Lys, I've just gotten word that Boston's had an accident and —" Jack said.

"Where is he?" she said, panicking that the love of her life was dying somewhere and she never had the courage to tell him how she really felt or that she forgave him.

"At the hospital, but —"

"I'm on my way."

"But Lys —"

Whatever her uncle was about to say was cut-off for good as she disconnected the call and rushed to find a taxi.

Tears streamed down her face as she silently prayed all the way while also hoping she'd reach Boston in time to tell him what was in her heart. She couldn't lose him. She just couldn't. Not when she had finally found the man of her dreams.

Rushing into the hospital and finding his room, she saw a person in the bed with bandages wrapped around his head. Heavy bruising also made his face unrecognisable. She was going to have to call Uncle Jack and tell him to come immediately since she wasn't sure if she could get through this alone.

The sight of Boston looking so fragile and hurt as he was hooked up to machines and drips had her emotions in turmoil. Sitting quietly beside him, she picked up his hand and began to speak.

"Bos, it's me. I know you don't like me for all the

horrible things I said and that you probably won't believe me, but I love you. Even though I didn't remember you I do remember the first time I saw you in the building foyer. It was such an incredibly magical moment I had forgotten even happened, but my subconscious must have known it was you as I trusted you from the first moment I woke up in the hospital," she said, tears streaming down her face. "I'm sorry for everything. For accusing you of not being you. I guess it was unbelievable that a complete and total stranger would give up a week of his life for me, which ended up with me falling in love with you. Please wake up. Let me love and take care of you for the rest of your life, no matter what." Wiping the tears away from her eyes, she closed them to pray he would be okay. "I'm not sure if you're family's been called, but if they haven't I'll do it and stay with you until they come."

"You know, I've heard stories about people going to hospitals and randomly sitting by patients hoping they'll wake up with amnesia," a male voice said, from behind her.

Her eyes opened with a start as her head whipped around in disbelief. The voice she just heard was Boston's.

"B-Boston?" she croaked, drinking in the sight of him, relief flooding through her that he was not only all right, but was now standing, albeit with crutches, in front of her. "I-if you're… T-then who…" Caught off guard and unable to get the words out coherently she immediately stood and took the opportunity he was holding crutches to hold his face and kiss him like she needed too. Tasting him, touching him, she felt her heart racing knowing this was where she was meant to be.

He was losing his balance because of the crutches, he told himself. Not because of Alyssa's kiss. God, he missed her so much and if he hadn't been such an idiot, then none of this would have happened.

Pulling apart they both smiled at each other.

"How, why are you here?" he said, easing himself back onto the bed with Alyssa's help, still unable to believe she was right here in front of him.

"Uncle Jack called to tell me that you were in an accident. I raced over to make sure that you were all right."

Boston didn't know how Jason knew Jack Lee, but smiled realising it could only have been Jason who told Jack he was here.

He silently thanked his meddling brother-in-law and Alyssa's uncle, but was also annoyed that Jack had worried Alyssa for nothing.

"Are you alright?" she said.

Seeing and hearing the concern on her face made him melt. This was the woman he wanted for the rest of his life.

"Yes, I'm fine. Just a badly sprained ankle."

"I'm so sorry," she said, bursting into tears.

"What? What for? If anyone should apologise, it's me.

I'm *sorry* for lying to you. I truly didn't mean for it happen, but I can't regret it either." Seeing Alyssa in tears tore at him, yet he didn't dare offer her comfort since there was only a very thin thread currently holding them together.

She knew exactly what he meant.

"I guess in some ways, you didn't really lie to me. It was more of a misunderstanding you didn't clear up," she said, magnanimous.

"I should have told you straight away that I didn't know you, but I was too chicken and thought you'd send me away. So I thought it would be easier to go with the lie. Unfortunately, you worked out the truth."

"I'm so sorry for accusing you of not being you," she said, wiping her eyes.

"Don't be. I understand. It must have freaked you out."

"It did." She nodded. "Then it got so confusing."

He didn't want to ask how she worked out he was now the *real* Boston however, a part of him needed to know.

"H-how did you find out I was, me?" he said, hesitant.

She shook her head still unable to believe her own stupidity.

"I found the other…" She couldn't bring herself to say Boston's name to refer to that fraud. "*Man's* wallet and after snooping, I saw his driver's licence wasn't the same name as I knew him. Then I found the fake business cards." Alyssa couldn't bring herself to tell Boston she had been going away with Keith at the time. "That's when

I realised the man I thought was you, wasn't you at all."

"Well, I'm just glad you know the truth."

Now was that awkward part where neither of them knew where they exactly stood.

"Did you mean it?" he said.

"Mean what?" she said, confused.

"What you said, just before I came in."

"Of course," she smiled. "The fact I was willing to tell a total stranger thinking it was you, should tell you something."

"Well, 'I' was all bandaged up and unconscious…" he teased. The smile on his face was like the sun had finally come out and her world of misery now gone.

She pulled the curtain so they could have some semblance of privacy.

"I love you, Lys."

"I love you too."

The smile and love on Boston's face was so glowing so bright, Alyssa felt basked in his love. This was the moment she knew beyond all doubt Boston was the one for her. The real Boston. Not some fake pretender.

* * * *

While the news didn't make headlines, it was known to only those who needed to know, that Triad boss Frankie Lee had died due to a car crash with his mistress. Lee's bodyguards, who were in the following car, said that some sort of fight must have occurred during the drive. They could only watch in horror as the car begin to swerve erratically along the road before going over the cliff and into deep bush before exploding.

Kai Kwong Lee was in Macau gambling and it was in the dead of night when he boarded his plane and headed to Singapore for business. By the time Kai returned to Hong Kong, no mention was ever made of an extra passenger who only travelled one way and was never seen again.

About the Author

Serena Black's love of reading romance novels, watching soap operas and rom-com TV shows and movies, opened her eyes to a world of romance that could be funny, adventurous, dramatic and sweet.

Now nothing makes her happier than to give readers the same bit of romantic escapism that culminates in happily ever after. No matter where her readers are, whether the day is wet and wintry or one for lazing on the beach, she hopes they pick up a book so that they might laugh, cry or even enjoy the arguments and always close the book with a loud romantic sigh.

Contact Serena at www.serenablackauthor.com.

Coming next:

Phoenix's story